Соня в царстве дива

Соня в царстве дива

THE FIRST RUSSIAN TRANSLATION
OF *ALICE'S ADVENTURES IN WONDERLAND*

by Lewis Carroll

WITH ILLUSTRATIONS BY
JOHN TENNIEL
AND BYRON W. SEWELL

INTRODUCTION AND NOTES BY
VICTOR FET

2017

Издательство/*Published by* Evertype, 73 Woodgrove, Portlaoise, R32 ENP6, Ireland. *www.evertype.com*.

Соня в царстве дива (Sonia v tsarstve diva). Название произведения в оригинале/*Original title*: *Alice's Adventures in Wonderland*. Автор/*Author*: *Льюис Кэрролл*/Lewis Carroll. Первое издание: Москва, Типография А. И. Мамонтова/*First edition* Moscow: Tipografiia A. I. Mamontova, 1879.

Издание первое/*First edition* 2017 г.

Каталожная запись этой книги доступна в Британской библиотеке.
A catalogue record for this book is available from the British Library.

ISBN-10 1-78201-198-6
ISBN-13 978-1-78201-198-9

Гарнитура De Vinne Text, Mona Lisa, ENGRAVERS' ROMAN, и *Liberty*. Набор Майкла Эверсона.
Typeset in De Vinne Text, Mona Lisa, ENGRAVERS' ROMAN, *and Liberty by* Michael Everson.

Иллюстрации на с./*Illustrations on pp.* 6, 8, 10, 14, 16, 18, 29, 30, 34, 37, 46, 48, 51, 52, 54, 57, 60, 62, 65, 68, 77, 79, 83, 88, 89, 91, 92, 93: *Джон Тенниел*/John Tenniel, 1865.
Иллюстрации на с./*Illustrations on pp.* 21, 23, 32, 70, 74: *Байрон В. Сьюэлл*/Byron W. Sewell, 2017.

Обложка/*Cover*: *Майкл Эверсон*/Michael Everson.

Печать/*Printed by* LightningSource.

Foreword

Once upon a time (say, most of the twentieth century and ours, up until 2013) there were only two known surviving copies of *Соня в царстве дива*, a small blue volume containing the first Russian translation of *Alice's Adventures in Wonderland*: one, er, salted away in the Saltykov-Shchedrin Library in St Petersburg, Russia, and the other bought by Alfred Berol, the pencil magnate, at Sotheby's in 1958, which ended up in the Berol Collection in the Fales Library of the Bobst Library at New York University.

Under the inspiration of my young daughter, Sonja (!), I arranged for a digital facsimile to be made, thanks to Marvin Taylor at NYU, which was published in hardcover by the Lewis Carroll Society of North America as a membership premium, with a simultaneous softcover trade edition by Michael Everson at Evertype. Included were my foreword; an introduction by the doyenne of Russian Carrollians, Nina Demurova; and an essay by Fan Parker. All research at the time pointed to one Olga Timiriaseff (Carroll's spelling; "Timiryazev" is a better transliteration) as the translator.

A few years later, Victor Fet, a Russian émigré and professor of Biology at Marshall University in Huntington, West Virginia, wrote to me saying he had some information about a far better candidate for the translator, Olga's cousin Ekaterina Timiryazev. His extensive research culminated in an article, "Around *Sonja*: On the First Russian Translation", published in our semiannual magazine,

Knight Letter (Vol. II, Issue 27, No. 97, Fall 2016), modified and included herein.

The year 2015 was an altogether remarkable one for Carrollians. Between its being the sesquicenTenniel (150th anniversary) of its publication, a weeklong conference in New York including a two-day seminar on translations, and the publication of the truly astonishing *Alice in a World of Wonderlands: The Translation of Lewis Carroll's Masterpieces* (Oak Knoll: Jon Lindseth, general editor, and Alan Tannenbaum, technical editor) in three volumes ("Essays", "Back Translations", "Checklists"), consisting of 2,656 pages covering 174 languages and dialects, it will long live in our memory.

Encouraged by all of these things—and the existence of a transcribed version online—it was decided by the three of us (Michael, Victor, and me) to produce a book that was different enough from the earlier *Соня* to justify its being a new volume, rather than an updated edition. This one has *Соня* typeset rather than in a facsimile, and contains all new essays and notes. The Tenniel illustrations have been restored to their rightful places, further adding to its cachet as the now definitive edition of *Соня*.

I believe Victor has done a great service to students, scholars, and other aficionados of Lewis Carroll in bringing to light a more probable translator, as well as his fastidious and meticulous, not to mention voluminous, research on the translation itself. Even for those of us who do not speak the Russian tongue but are fascinated by the translation process, there is plenty here to read and to get excited about.

Mark Burstein
President Emeritus
The Lewis Carroll Society of North America
Petaluma, California

Introduction

This is the first reprinting of *Соня в царстве дива* (*Sonia v tsarstve diva*) in modern Russian orthography. The text is based on the original *Соня въ царствѣ дива* (*Sonia v tsarstvie diva*, 1879) reprinted as a facsimile (2013).[1] I am grateful to Sergey Kuriy (Сергей Курий, Kiev, Ukraine), who has produced a version of this text in modern Russian orthography and made it available online on his great Carrollian website.[2] I further proofed and corrected this text, and formatted its paragraphs to follow Carroll's original text.

The Russian spelling, grammar, and punctuation have changed considerably since the 1870s. In the orthographic reform of 1918, the Russian alphabet lost some letters, most notably the letter *ять* (*yat'*, ѣ), the letter i, and the terminal letter hard sign (ъ) was dropped. In this edition, spelling and grammar are modified to conform to the modern Russian norms, except in a few cases mentioned below. This edition, like other Evertype editions, is consistent in its use of the Russian letter *ё* (*yo*), which has an ambiguous status in Russian orthography.

1 Carroll, Lewis. 2013. *Соня въ царствѣ дива: Sonja in a Kingdom of Wonder*. A facsimile of the first Russian translation of *Alice's Adventures in Wonderland*. [s.l.]: Lewis Carroll Society of North America, ISBN 978-0-30326-00-5 (hardback, black and white); Cathair na Mart: Evertype, ISBN 978-1-78201-040-1 (paperback, colour).

2 www.kursivom.ru.

The original 1879 text was rather poorly proofed, and has spelling, punctuation, and even grammatical errors; quotation marks are not closed, etc. All such obvious errors are corrected in this edition. In capitalizing the names of the characters we have favoured Carroll's own practice, since capitalization in the original text was not consistent: *Беленький/Белый Кролик* (*Belen'kii/Belyi Krolik* 'White Rabbit'), *Мышь* (*Mysh'* 'Mouse'), *Утка* (*Utka* 'Duck'), *Попугай* (*Popugay* 'Parrot'), *Журавль* (*Zhuravl'* 'Crane'), *Орлёнок* (*Orlënok* 'Eaglet'), *Жаба* (*Zhaba* 'Toad'), *Сорока* (*Soroka* 'Magpie'), *Канарейка* (*Kanareyka* 'Canary'), *Червяк* (*Cherviak* 'Caterpillar'), *Голубка* (*Golubka* 'Dove'), *Лакей-Рыба* (*Lakey-Ryba* 'Fish-Footman'), *Лакей-Лягушка* (*Lakey-Liagushka* 'Frog-Footman'), *Червонная Краля* (*Chervonnaia Kralia*, 'Queen of Hearts'), *Пиковая Княгиня* (*Pikovaia Kniaginia* 'The Duchess'), *Сибирская Кошка/Киска* (*Sibirskaia Koshka/ Kiska*, 'Cheshire-Cat'), *Заяц* (*Zaiats* 'Hare'), *Грифон* (*Grifon*, 'Gryphon'), and *Телячья Головка* (*Teliach'ia Golovka* 'Mock Turtle').

The translation is abridged, especially heavily in the end. A considerable portion of Carroll's puns and parody poetry was left out. The translation had ten chapters instead of twelve since it fused Carroll's Chapters IX and X and Chapters XI and XII. In this edition, since it is quite clear where the fusion occurs, the first half of the 1879 chapter "Соня в зверинце" ("Sonia v zverintse", 'Sonia in a Menagerie') has been retained as Chapter IX, with its second half titled here "Раковая пляска" ("Rakovaia pliaska", 'The Lobster Dance') as Chapter X; the first part of "Заседание суда" ("Zasedanie suda" 'The Trial') remains as Chapter XI, with newly titled "Показания Сони" ("Pokazaniia Soni" 'Sonia's Evidence') split off as Chapter XII.

Only 16 of the Tenniel illustrations were used in the original edition, after carefully removing Tenniel's initials and the Dalziels' monograms, in an evident attempt to conceal the English origin of the book, which bore no names of the author, translator, or illustrator (see "Sonia's Adventures", below, p. xxix). In this edition, 17 of Tenniel's original 42 illustrations have been added to the 16 because they contained vignettes which still remain in the book. Some of these, however, were modified: the publisher and I are grateful to have had our friend and colleague Byron W. Sewell re-draw five of them, since the translator changed the Dodo and flamingo to cranes, Bill the Lizard to Vas′ka the Cockroach, and made a hedgehog more prominent.

One error in zoology made by the translator has been corrected. In Chapter III, Carroll has a young Crab speak to its mother; in the 1879 translation (p. 36, p. 25 here), a young Frog speaks to a Toad, but as the familial relation is still apparent and frogs and toads are different species, the latter has been used for both.

On p. 72 of the original (p. 45 here), there is an added footnote explaining the word "croquet" as 'a ball game, a kind of lawn billiard'. The footnote of course is absent in Lewis Carroll's *Wonderland*.

There is a case of spelling in Chapter XI (p. 87), which is retained here as in the original 1879 text. Alice called the Jurors "stupid things", and one of them, as we know, did not know how to spell the word "stupid". The Russian translator extended Carroll's pun as allowed in a language with a grammatical gender for the adjectives; a correct *глупыя* (*glupyia*, plural feminine) vs. an incorrect *глупые* (*glupye*, plural masculine). However, this distinction works only if one follows the 19th-century spelling, because after the 1918 reform, *glupye* was adopted for both cases. In Kuriy's online text, the pun is *reversed* to fit modern orthography norms, i.e., *glupye* is treated as correct. A variety of notes and glosses relevant to the understanding of obscure words or idioms has been included at the end of the text.

Victor Fet
Huntington, West Virginia
February 2017

Sonia's Adventures: The First Russian Translation of *Wonderland*[3]

The first Russian translation of *Wonderland* was published anonymously in 1879 as *Sonia v tsarstvie diva* (*Sonia in a Kingdom of Wonder*), hereinafter referred to as *Sonia*.[4] Deep Victorian mysteries surround it. Its translator remains unknown—but a hint from Lewis Carroll himself leads one to Russian aristocrats, patrons of the arts, and famous writers. Its readership is undocumented, but the faces of children who most likely first read this book are still well known in Russia today, having been painted by the most famous nineteenth-century Russian artists. Further, as one looks carefully at the text itself, one finds it remarkably interesting, even by today's standards.

As mentioned, Lewis Carroll was not acknowledged as the author of *Sonia*. The book reproduced only sixteen of Tenniel's illustrations and received very negative reviews. (The four known surviving reviews are reprinted below, from p. xxxiv in Russian

3 An earlier version of this essay was published in the *Knight Letter*, Fall 2016, Vol. II, Issue 37, No 97: 25–34.

4 *Соня въ царствѣ дива*. Москва: Типографія А. И. Мамонтова, 1879, 166 с. (*Sonia v tsarstvie diva / Sonia in a Kingdom of Wonder*. Moscow: Tipografiia A. I. Mamontova, 1879, 166 pp.) (in Russian).

and from p. xl in English.) The book apparently was so thoroughly forgotten that the next time it was mentioned in Russia was in the late 1960s.

Sonia is considerably abridged and heavily "domesticated," that is, all English names and context markers were removed, and all characters were "Russified". This was discussed in the 2013 facsimile edition of *Sonia*, published simultaneously by the LCSNA as a limited-distribution hardback (with greyscale images of the facsimile), and by Evertype as a paperback (with colour images of the facsimile).[5] It features commentaries by Fan Parker and Nina Demurova.[6, 7] This pioneering practice of "domestication" was also used in later Russian translations—of which Nabokov's *Аня в Стране чудес* ("*Ania v Strane chudes*" 'Anya in Wonderland', 1923) is the best known.

There are only two known surviving copies of *Sonia*.[8] One survived, unnoticed, in the Saltykov-Shchedrin Library in St. Petersburg, Russia. August A. Imholtz, Jr. managed to obtain its microfilm, and a scanned file is now available online. The second—the only known copy outside of Russia—surfaced in 1958 at Sotheby's. It went to the Alfred Berol Carroll collection, now at New York University's Fales Library. Its title page was reproduced in 1995 by Nina Demurova.[9] (The Fales copy was the source for the 2013 reprinting.) NYU has a digitized version of it. There was also a third copy in the Russian State (formerly Lenin)

5 [Carroll, Lewis]. 2013. *Соня въ царствѣ дива: Sonja in a Kingdom of Wonder*. A facsimile of the first Russian translation of *Alice's Adventures in Wonderland*. [s.l.]: Lewis Carroll Society of North America, ISBN 978-0-30326-00-5 (hardback, black and white); Cathair na Mart: Evertype, ISBN 978-1-78201-040-1 (paperback, colour), 177 pp.

6 Parker, Fan. "The first translation", in *Sonja v tsarstvie diva*, 2013, pp. 169–172. Reprinted from: Parker, F. *Lewis Carroll in Russia: Translations of Alice in Wonderland, 1879–1979*. Russian House Ltd, 1994, 89 pp.

7 Demurova, Nina M. "Sonja and Napoleon: The first Russian translation", in *Sonja v tsarstvie diva*, 2013, pp. X–XV.

8 Imholtz, August A., Jr. and Imholtz, Clare. "Alice goes to Russia", in *Slavic & East European Information Resources*, 2014, 15: 150–160.

9 Demurova, Nina M. "Alice speaks Russian: the Russian translations of *Alice's Adventures in Wonderland* and *Through the Looking-Glass*", in *Harvard Library Bulletin*, 1994-1995, 5(4): 11–29 (Aug. 1995).

Library in Moscow that was discarded or stolen in 1979, though a microfilm survives. *Sonia* has not been reprinted in Russia, but the text was made available online (both in old and in modern spelling).

The Fales copy of *Sonia* has, on its second fly-leaf, a pencil inscription in Italian (!): *Sofia nel regno de meraviglie*, possibly identifying it as *Wonderland* (which is obvious from Tenniel's illustrations even to someone who does not read Russian). Sotheby's staff kindly informed us that this book originated from Davis & Orioli, a London bookseller. Giuseppe "Pino" Orioli (1884–1942) was a Florentine and London bookseller, a partner of the writer Norman Douglas, known as a publisher of controversial literature such as D. H. Lawrence's *Lady Chatterley's Lover* (1928). An additional mark on the fly-leaf reads "4-25", which could mean April 1925; the copy could have been obtained by Orioli in Italy after the Russian Revolution of 1917, and brought over with an émigré library; a large expatriate Russian community existed in Florence.

At least four reviews of *Sonia* appeared in Russian periodicals between 1879 and 1882.[10, 11] These reviews are decidedly negative and even indignant. One of the reviewers, M. V. Sobolev, a children's literature expert of that time,[12] opined that "the morality is overexaggerated, and … Sonia's adventures are hardly interesting." None of the reviewers recognized that the book was a translation, nor did they identify it as Carroll's *Alice*! This

10 Рушайло, А. М. "Время собирать книги", in *Библиография*, 1995, 4(272): 88–98 (Rushaylo, A. M., "Vremia sobirat′ knigi" / "Time to collect books", in *Bibliografiia*, 1995, 4[272]: 88–98, in Russian).

11 Лобанов, В. В. *Льюис Кэрролл в России*. (Lobanov, V. V., *L'iuis Kérroll v Rossii / Lewis Carroll in Russia*. Annotated bibliography of translations.) *Folia Anglistica*, Autumn 2000; Moscow: Maks-Press, 2000 (in Russian).

12 Белоусов, А. Ф., О. А. Лучкина, И. А. Сергиенко, В. В. Головин и С. Г. Маслинская. "Критика детской литературы 1864–1934: фрагмент аннотированного указателя", in *Детские чтения*, 2015, 8(2): 7–29 (Belousov, A. F., O. A. Luchkina, I. A. Sergienko, V. V. Golovin and S. G. Maslinskaia. "Kritika detskoi literatury 1864–1934: fragment annotirovannogo ukazatelia" / "The criticism of children's literature in 1864–1934: a fragment of an annotated index", in *Detskie chteniia / Children Readings*), 2015, 8(2): 7–29 (in Russian).

demonstrates just how unfamiliar the Russians were with Carroll at that time.

There are several alternative transliterations of *Соня*: *Sonya*, *Sonia*, and *Soni͡a*. In this volume, we use the transliteration "Sonia" unless referring to the 2013 reprinting where "Sonja" has been used. This name, a diminutive of Sofia, also means 'a sleepy-head' in Russian (from *son*, "a dream") and was clearly chosen to indicate Alice's dream (unlike Nabokov's Anya, which has no secondary meaning). "Sonia" also means 'dormouse'; this noun in Russian has a feminine gender, and therefore the Dormouse is usually a female (but in *Sonia*, it was replaced by a male, *Mishen'ka-Surok*, 'Mishen'ka the Marmot').

Warren Weaver, who studied Carroll's correspondence with his publisher, Macmillan, wrote in his book *Alice in Many Tongues* (p. 47): "On March 31, 1871, occurs a Dodgson letter of special interest: 'Unless it should happen that I have already given the order, will you please send a French and a German *Alice* to Miss Timiriasef—care of the Rev. H. S. Thompson, English Church, St. Petersburg. She is the lady who, I believe, is going to translate *Alice* into Russian.'"[13] Cohen and Gandolfo reprinted the same letter (p. 90), but with the spelling "Timiriaseff", and the sentence ending "… is going to translate *Alice* into Russian for me."[14] This letter by Carroll, in fact, is the earliest documented evidence that *Wonderland* was known to anyone in Russia. The very first mention in print I could find of *Alice* books (both *Wonderland* and *Looking-Glass*) in Russia was in 1883, in a translation of an 1881 essay by British children's writer Anna Jane Buckland.[15]

13 Weaver, Warren. *Alice in Many Tongues*. Madison: The University of Wisconsin Press, 1964.

14 Cohen, Morton and Gandolfo, Anita, eds. *Lewis Carroll and the House of Macmillan*. Cambridge University Press, 1987, p. 90.

15 Buckland, Anna J. "On stories in the kindergarten", in *Essays on the Kindergarten, Being a Selection of Lectures Read before the London Froebel Society*. London: Sonnenschein & Allen, 1881, pp. 19–35. Translated into Russian as: Бекленд, А. "О пользе рассказов в детском саду", in *Народная школа*, 1883, 6: 22–36 (Beklend, A. "O pol'ze rasskazov v detskom sadu", in *Narodnaia shkola / People's School*), 1883, 6: 22–36.

Neither the Rev. Thompson nor Miss Timiriaseff were mentioned in Carroll's diaries or his *Russian Journal*, the 1867 travelogue of his continental journey.[16] Discussing the copy of *Sonia* sold at Sotheby's in 1958, Weaver made a connection with Miss Timiriaseff: "Can it be that she is the translator of the 1879 edition?" The Russian scholar Dmitrii Urnov mused:

> So who was [the translator]? Possibly, Olga Ivanovna Timiryazeva, a first cousin of the famous scientist K. A. Timiryazev. Her brother left memoirs where he tells about his family that was friendly with Pushkin, about him and his sister reading as children in major European languages including English, while their readings were selected by [the famous poet Vasily] Zhukovsky himself. Indeed, *Sonia v tsarstve diva* falls within the tradition of the Russian or translated literary fairy tale that was created for us by Pushkin and Zhukovsky.[17]

Urnov's suggestion, first made in 1975, became the source of further attribution, usually with a question mark. The suggestion, however, was based exclusively on Carroll's letter quoted by Weaver, which then became known in Russia. Demurova mentions that Weaver sent her a copy of his 1964 book after her translations of both *Alice* books were published (1967).[18] No further inquiry, to my knowledge, has been made into the identity of the putative translator.

16 Кэрролл, Л. *Дневник путешествия в Россию в 1867 г. Статьи и эссе о Льюисе Кэрролле.* Челябинск: Энциклопедия; С.-Петербург: Крига, 2013, 415 с. (Kérroll, L. *Dnevnik puteshestviia v Rossiiu v 1867 g., ili Russkii dnevnik. Stat'i i ésse o L'iuise Kérolle.* / Carroll, L. *Journal of a tour in Russia in 1867. Articles and Essays about Lewis Carroll.* Chelyabinsk: Entsiklopediia; St. Petersburg: Kriga, 2013, 415 pp., in Russian).

17 Урнов, Д., с. 225 в кн.: Винтерих, Д. *Приключения знаменитых книг.* 3-е изд. Москва: Книга, 1985. Предисловие, послесловие, комментарии Д. Урнова (Первое изд., 1975) (Urnov, D., p. 225 in: Vinterikh, D. *Prikliucheniia znamenitykh knig / The Adventures of the Famous Books.* (Abridged transl. by E. Skvairs of: Winterich, J. *Books and the Man.* NY: Greenberg, 1929). 3d Ed. Moscow: Kniga, 1985. Foreword, afterword, commentaries by D. Urnov, in Russian; first ed. 1975).

18 Кэрролл, Л., op. cit.

The "Timiriaseff" family name is well known in Russia due to the famous biologist Kliment Arkadyevich Timiryazev (1843–1920), a scion of the old aristocracy, who after 1917 supported the Bolshevik regime. Information about his cousin Olga Ivanovna Timiryazeva (1841–1897) is scarce. Olga's brother Fëdor (1832–1897) was a governor of Saratov in 1880–1881, and published a memoir to which Urnov refers.[19] During her youth in Moscow in the early 1860s, Olga Timiryazeva was a piano student of the famous composer Nikolay Rubinstein (1835–1881). She belonged to the circle of Prince Vladimir Odoevsky (1803–1869), a famous polymath and philosopher; Olga is mentioned many times in his diaries. Odoevsky was among those writers who brought the European literary fairytale style to Russia; his *Gorodok v tabakerke* ('A Town in a Snuffbox') (1832) was written in the tradition of E. T. A. Hoffmann. In 1866, Olga Timiryazeva was appointed a lady-in-waiting (*фрейлина, freylina*) to the Empress Maria Alexandrovna (1824–1880), the consort of Alexander II, so from 1866 she lived in St. Petersburg, which matches Dodgson's letter of 1871. She was still listed as a *freylina* (that is, she remained unmarried) at the coronation of Nicholas II in 1896.

So far I have found no evidence that Olga Timiryazeva ever published any literary work. However, I was able to locate *another* "Miss Timiriaseff" who also lived at the same time in St. Petersburg, and developed into a well-known translator. She was Kliment's niece, Ekaterina Ivanovna Timiryazeva (1848–1921), better known under her married surname, Boratynskaya.[20] In

19 Тимирязев, Ф. И. "Страницы прошлого", in *Русский архив*, 1884, 1(1): 155–180, (2): 298–330 (Timiryazev, F. I. "Stranitsy proshlogo" / "Pages from the Past", in *Russkii arkhiv / The Russian Archive*, 1884, 1(1): 155–180, (2): 298–330 (in Russian).

20 Лукьянов, С. М. *О Вл. Соловъёве в его молодые годы: материалы к биографии*. Москва: Книга, 1990, т. 3, 381 с. (Lukyanov, S. M. *O Vl. Solovyove v ego molodye gody: materialy k biografii / On Vl. Solovyov in His Youth: Materials for a Biography.*) Moscow: Kniga, 1990, vol. 3, 381 pp.) (in Russian). Pp. 8-12 and 20-29 in this book include memoirs of Ekaterina Ivanovna Boratynskaya (née Timiryazeva) as told by her to S. M. Lukyanov in 1918. Some sources give her birth date as 1852 but in her memoirs E. I. B. says that she was born on 25 December 1847 (Old Style) (=6 January 1848, New Style). She was home-schooled and lived with her grandmother in St.

February 1871, she married Lev Andreevich Boratynsky (1849–1907), from 1890 the Vice Governor of Moscow, but their marriage did not last. Ekaterina Ivanovna Boratynskaya pursued a pedagogical career; from 1880 to 1917 she served as an assistant principal of the Alexandro-Mariinskaia Women School, a charity institution for poor girls. In 1896–1897, we see her living in an apartment full of books, giving lessons to seven-year-old Boris Pasternak (1890–1960). The great Russian poet affectionately remembered Boratynskaya as his first teacher.[21]

Unlike Olga (who was her father's first cousin), Ekaterina Boratynskaya became an accomplished author and translator from English and French, including children's and art literature. Many of her translations were signed only by the initials "E.B." She left memoirs about the famous religious philosopher Vladimir Solovyov (1853–1900);[22] she was a friend of the lyric poet Afanasii Fet, and a very close friend and collaborator of Lev (Leo) Tolstoy. (Most likely it was through Tolstoy that Boratynskaya met Pasternak's parents and became his home teacher.) Boratynskaya contributed translations for Tolstoy's publishing house, Posrednik ("The Mediator"), beginning in 1891. The chief editor of *Posrednik* remembered Ekaterina Boratynskaya as one of the most active contributors.[23] She translated and retold an incredibly diverse

Petersburg until age 23, when she married L.A. Boratynsky (then a graduate student in Moscow University) on 30 January 1871 (Old Style = 11 February 1871, New Style).

21 Pasternak, Boris. *I Remember: Sketch for an Autobiography* (transl. by D. Magarshak). NY: Pantheon, 1959, p. 33: "Of all these teachers, whom I remember with gratitude, I shall mention my first teacher, Yekaterina Ivanovna Baratynskaya, a writer of children's stories and a translator of children's books from the English. She taught me reading and writing, elementary arithmetics and French, starting from the very beginning, that is, how to sit on a chair and how to hold a pen in my hand… . ". – Смолицкий, В. Г. *«Я жил в те дни...» Биографические этюды о Борисе Пастернаке.* Москва: Роза и крест, 2012. (Smolitsky, V.G. "*Ya zhil v te dni…" Biograficheskie étiudy o Borise Pasternake. / "I lived in those days…" Biographical etudes about Boris Pasternak.* Moscow: Roza i krest, 2012).

22 Лукьянов, С. М., op. cit.

23 Горбунов-Посадов, И. И. "О моих учителях и товарищах по работе", in *Сорок лет служения людям.* Москва, 1925 (Gorbunov-Posadov, I. I.

НОВЫЯ ИЗДАНІЯ

„ПОСРЕДНИКА",

„Библіотеки И. И. Горбунова-Посадова

ДЛЯ ДѢТЕЙ И ЮНОШЕСТВА"

СИРОТКА ГЕРТИ и другіе разсказы Виктора Гюго, Джоржа Хиса, А. М. Коммейсъ и другихъ. Со многими рисунками. Въ хромолитогр. обложкѣ. М. 1903 г. Ц. 1 руб., въ папкѣ 1 р. 25 к.

ЧУДНЫЙ ДАРЪ. Сборникъ сказокъ Виктора Гюго, Лабуле, Франсуа Коппе, Джона Рёскина, Эжезиппа Моро и Кармень Сильвы. Съ 25 рисунками. Въ хромолитогр. обложкѣ. М. 1903 г. Ц. 75 коп., въ папкѣ 1 руб.

СЕРДЦЕ БѢДНЫХЪ. Разсказы Э. Демольдера. Съ французскаго. Переводъ Сергѣя Орловскаго. Съ рисунками Кутюрье. М. 1903 г. Ц. 60 к., въ папкѣ 80 к.

КАПИТАНЪ ЯНВАРЬ. Разсказъ. Съ англійскаго перевела Е. Б. Съ рисунками. М. 1904 г.

ВЕСЕЛАЯ РѢЧКА, ИЛИ ТИМОШИНЫ ПОИСКИ. Разсказъ для каждаго, молодого или стараго, кто пожелаетъ его прочесть. Соч. Кэтъ Дугласъ-Виггинъ. Съ рисунками Оливера Герфорда. Съ англійскаго перевела Е. Б. Москва. 1901 г. Ц. 50 к., въ папкѣ 70 к.

СЧАСТЬЕ БѢДНАГО МАЛЫША. Разсказъ Кэтъ Дугласъ-Виггинъ. Съ англійскаго перев. Е. Б. Съ 6-ю рисунками. Москва. 1901 г. Ц. 25 к., въ папкѣ 35 к.

ЗОЛОТЫЕ КУДРИ. Повѣсть Джоржа Элліотъ. Съ рисунками Реджинальда Берча. Съ англійскаго Е. Б. Москва. 1901 г. Ц. 70 к., въ папкѣ 90 к.

ШКОЛЬНЫЕ ТОВАРИЩИ. Эдмондо д'Амичиса. Переводъ съ итальянск. А. Ульяновой. Съ предисловіемъ И. Горбунова-Посадова. Съ рисунками. Изд. 2-е. Москва. 1901 г. Ц. 85 к., въ папкѣ 1 р. 10 к., въ переплетѣ 1 р. 50 к.

КРАСАВЕЦЪ ДЖОЙ. Исторія собаки, разсказанная ею самой. Маршаль Саундерсъ. Съ англійскаго перевела Е. Б. Съ рисунками. Москва. 1901 г. Ц. 60 коп., въ папкѣ 80 к., въ переплетѣ 1 р. 10 к.

МАЙСКІЙ ЦВѢТОКЪ. Сборникъ разсказовъ. Съ рисунками. Въ хромолитографированной обложкѣ. Москва. 1902 г. Ц. 55 к., въ папкѣ 75 к. *Содержаніе:* Майскій цвѣтокъ. Разсказъ Кэтъ Дугласъ-Виггинъ. Найденышъ. Разсказъ Альфонса Додэ, съ французскаго. Сидѣлка. По Франсуа Коппе. Нелло и Патрашъ. Разсказъ Уйда, съ англійскаго.

array of English, American, and French literature for children, including *Uncle Tom's Cabin*, Longfellow's "Evangeline," stories

"O moikh uchiteliakh i tovarishchakh po rabote" / "On my teachers and coworkers", in *Sorok let sluzheniia liudiam / Forty Years of Service to the People*, Moscow, 1925 (in Russian). See above for some translations by Posrednik, including those by "Е. Б." (= E. Boratynskaya).

of Ernest Thompson Seton, *Black Beauty* by Anna Sewell, *The Lamplighter* by Maria S. Cummins, George Eliot's *Adam Bede* and *Silas Marner, Timothy's Quest* by Kate Douglas Wiggin, *Captain January* by Laura E. Richards, *Beautiful Joe* by Margaret Marshall Saunders, and *Cosette* (a fragment from Hugo's *Les Miserables*). On Tolstoy's suggestion, she translated Alice Bunker Stockham's *Creative Life: A Special Letter to Young Girls* (1893), an early text on woman health. It is quite possible that the Macmillan books in 1871 were requested for the young Ekaterina Timiryazeva rather than for Olga.

Note that Carroll asked specifically for French and German, but not English, texts of *Wonderland* (both the first translations, just published by Macmillan in 1869) to be sent to a "Miss Timiriaseff". The request (which can be dated by 1870) meant that she wanted to read *Alice* in more familiar languages (although there is no doubt that *Sonia* was translated from English.) Educated Russians usually had good French and German, but English was much less common.

At the same time, English was spoken by the Timiryazev family branch in St. Petersburg, which had unusually close historical ties with England. Ekaterina's grandmother (and Kliment's mother) was Baroness Adelaida Klementyevna Timiryazeva (née de Bode) who considered herself an Englishwoman. Adelaida's grandmother, Mary Kinnersley of Staffordshire, married a French officer, Baron de Bode; they settled in Alsace but after the French Revolution fled to Russia. Ekaterina Boratynskaya wrote that she lived with Adelaida since age 10 (that is, from 1858), and that their home environment was rather Protestant than Russian Orthodox.[24] It is likely that they had connections to the English expatriate community.

This might explain why in his 1871 letter, Carroll asked Macmillan to send *Wonderland* to "Miss Timiriaseff" c/o "Rev. H. S. Thompson, English Church, St. Petersburg."[25, 26] We assume that the Timiryazevs learned about *Wonderland* from this

24 Лукьянов, С. М., op. cit.

25 Weaver, W., op. cit.

26 Cohen, M. and Gandolfo, A., op. cit.

clergyman, who therefore would have possessed an English copy. However, the Rev. Thompson's first initial should be A, not H. (Possibly an error on Carroll's part based on the name of his old friend, Henry L. Thompson of Christ Church?) In 1864–1877, the Anglican chaplain in St. Petersburg was Arthur Steinkopff Thompson (1835–1919), who also served as a chaplain of the British embassy. While Thompson is not mentioned in Carroll's diaries or his *Russian Journal*, the 1867 travelogue mentions his two colleagues, the Rev. Robert George Penney (1838–1912) in Moscow, and the Rev. John H. Herbert McSwiney (1827–1899), a chaplain of the British consulate in Cronstadt (the naval fortress off St. Petersburg). Both Penney and McSwiney hosted and guided Carroll and his traveling companion, Henry Liddon, during their tour; the Rev. Penney visited Dodgson in Oxford in June 1886.[27] Interestingly, McSwiney's uncle, Thomas Robert Allfree (1788–1868) served in Russia in the 1820s–1830s and taught English to the Grand Dukes (future Alexander II and his brother Nicholas; their principal tutor was the poet Zhukovsky).

Arthur S. Thompson was a son of the famous Victorian physician Theophilus Thompson (1807–1860). After his return to England in 1877, Thompson was a vicar in several parishes, and an active member of the Anglo-Russian Literary Society; he published such titles as *Home Words for Wanderers* and *Sermons Preached Abroad to English Worshippers*. He was mentioned briefly in connection with Arthur Penrhyn Stanley, the Dean of Westminster,[28] as they both officiated in St. Petersburg on 23 January 1874 at the wedding of Prince Alfred, Duke of Edinburgh (Queen Victoria's second son) and the Grand Duchess Maria, the only daughter of Alexander II.

Interestingly, the Rev. Thompson's wife was Ellen Jameson (1843–1878), whose brother, the Rev. Kingsbury Jameson, in 1881 married Grace MacDonald (1854–1884), daughter of Lewis Carroll's most important mentor, George MacDonald (1824–

27 Кэрролл, Л., op. cit.

28 *The American Annual Cyclopedia and Register of Important Events*, 14 (1874), p. 765. NY: Appleton & Co., 1875.

1905). It was MacDonald who, with enthusiastic support of his children, convinced Carroll to submit *Wonderland* for publication.

Sonia was published in Moscow by Anatoly Mamontov (1839–1905).[29, 30] He is much less well known than his brother, Savva Mamontov (1840–1918), who was called "Savva the Magnificent" and was the most famous Russian patron of the arts at the time. *The Bloomsbury Guide to Art* summarizes:

> After making his fortune by building the first railway from Archangel to Murmansk, [Mamontov] bought the Abramtsevo estate near Moscow in 1870. In 1872 he invited the landscape painter Vasily Polenov and the sculptor [Mark] Antokolsky… to Abramtsevo as the basis of an artistic colony, and they were later joined by Repin and the brothers Viktor and Apollinarius Vasnetsov. The estate became a focus for the revival in traditional Russian arts and crafts.… The Abramtsevo artists also contributed ornate set and costume designs to Mamontov's amateur dramatics; and when he founded his own stage and theatre companies, these greatly influenced theatre design in Russia.[31]

Much has been written about the Mamontov Artistic Circle.[32, 33] Many other great names were associated with them, such as the

29 Бокман, Г. "Анатолий и Михаил Мамонтовы как типографы и издатели", in *Иерусалимский библиофил*, 4. Иерусалим: Филобиблон, 2011. (Bokman, G. "Anatolii i Mikhail Mamontovy kak tipografy i izdateli" / "Anatoly and Mikhail Mamontov as printers and publishers", in *Ierusalimskii bibliofil / The Jerusalem Bibliophile*. No 4. Jerusalem: Filobiblon, 2011, in Russian).

30 Полиновская, Л. Д. "Московский типограф Анатолий Иванович Мамонтов и его связи с общественно-политическим движением в России", in *Книга: Исследования и материалы*. Москва, 1990, 60: 132–140 (Polinovskaia, L. D. "Moskovskii tipograf Anatoly Ivanovich Mamontov i ego sviazi s obshchestvenno-politicheskim dvizheniem v Rossii" / "The Moscow publisher Anatoly Ivanovich Mamontov and his connections to the social-political movement in Russia", in *Kniga: Issledovaniia i materialy / The Book: Studies and Materials*. Moscow, 1990, 60: 132–140, in Russian).

31 West, Shearer. *The Bloomsbury Guide to Art*. London: Bloomsbury Publishing PLC, 1996.

painters Valentin Serov, Konstantin Korovin, and Mikhail Vrubel; the opera singer Feodor Chaliapin; and the stage director Konstantin Stanislavsky.

The family of *Sonia*'s publisher was also part of this greater Mamontov clan. Anatoly Ivanovich Mamontov opened his printing house in Moscow in 1863. In 1873, he added a book-and-toy store named *Detskoe vospitanie* ("Children's Education") where *Sonia* was sold. (We know this from one of the reviews that included bookstore advertisement information; see below). The bookstore was owned by Anatoly's wife, Maria Alexandrovna Mamontova (née Lyalina, 1847–1904). There, she later organized a toy shop to make dolls in folk dresses for the first time in Russia. Her niece Maria Morozova (1878–1958) remembered: "It was such a charming store, which had everything you could think about! M. A. herself was always there, and enthusiastically demonstrated all the toys invented by her. Both children and adults loved the wonderful small world she created—everything there was so pretty and entertaining; she had so much taste and fantasy."[34] The famous *matrëshka*, or nested doll, emerged from this store in 1898—a cultural fusion of Russian and Japanese woodcarving. Today, one remembers Maria Mamontova's name mostly in connection with this doll, but she also published collections of children stories and games starting from 1870.[35, 36] As early as 1872, she published a

32 Арензон, Е. *Савва Мамонтов*. Москва: Русская книга, 1995 (Arenzon, E. *Savva Mamontov*. Moscow: Russkaia kniga, 1995, in Russian).

33 Haldey, Olga. *Mamontov's Private Opera: The Search for Modernism in Russian Theater*, 2010, Bloomington: Indiana University Press.

34 Морозова, М. К. "'Мои воспоминания': Публикация Е. М. Буромской-Морозовой", in *Наше наследие*, 1991, 6(24): 89-109 (Morozova, M. K. "Moi vospominaniia" / "'My memoirs': Publication by E. M. Buromskaiia-Morozova", in *Nashe nasledie / Our Heritage*, 1991, 6(24): 89-109, in Russian).

35 Anon., *Рассказы для маленьких детей*. Москва: Типография А. И. Мамонтова, 1870, 138 с. (*Rasskazy dlia malen'kikh detei / Stories for the Little Children*). Moscow: Tipografiia A. I. Mamontova, 1870, 138 pp. (in Russian)

36 Мамонтова, М. А. и Соловьёва, М. Т. *Детские игры и песни*. Москва: Детский сад М. Т. Соловьёвой, 1872, 87 с. (Mamontova, M. A. and Solovyova, M. T. *Detskie igry i pesni / Children's Games and Songs*. Moscow:

song collection with music arranged by no less than Tchaikovsky.[37] In 1881, she launched a children's magazine, *Detskii otdykh* ("Children's Pastime").

Who were *Sonia*'s first young readers in Russia? So far I have not found the book mentioned in any diaries or memoirs; however, one can reasonably assume that Maria Mamontova's children made good use of their mother's bookstore! A shortlist of "the children who likely read *Sonia*" includes 15 names (nine girls and six boys): the six children of Anatoly and Maria and their nine first cousins (children of Anatoly's brothers, Savva and Fëdor).

The faces of some of these children will be known to almost any educated Russian today: Over the years, the most famous Abramtsevo artists—Valentin Serov, Ilya Repin, Viktor Vasnetsov, and others—painted portraits of the Mamontovs, adults and children alike. Vera Savvichna Mamontova (b. 1875), the publisher's niece, was portrayed as *Девочка с персиками / Devochka s persikami* (*'Girl with the Peaches'*) by Serov (1887)—probably *the* best-known Russian girl's portrait (Fig. 1 on the following page). Also shown here are images of Sofia Fëdorovna Mamontova, another of the publisher's nieces (Fig. 2, by Repin, 1879) and Ludmila Anatolyevna Mamontova, the publisher's daughter (*Портрет Милуши / Portret Milushi* (*'A Portrait of Milusha'*); the first serious portrait done by the 19-year-old Serov in 1884) (Fig. 3). Ludmila's sisters Tatyana (Fig. 4) and Natalya were the models for Vasnetsov's fairy-tale painting, *Иван-Царевич на Сером Волке / Ivan-Tsarevich na Serom Volke* ("Prince Ivan on the Grey Wolf," 1889) (Fig. 5).

Detskii sad M. T. Solovyovoy / M. T. Solovyova's Kindergarten, 1872, 87 pp., in Russian).

37 Мамонтова, М. А. и Чайковский, П. И. *Детские песни на русские и малороссийские напевы с аккомпанементом фортепиано.* Типография А. И. Мамонтова, 1872, 56 с. (2-е изд. 1875) (Mamontova, M. A. and Tchaikovsky, P. I. *Detskie pesni na russkie i malorossiiskie napevy s akkompanementom fortepiano. / Children's songs on Russian and Ukrainian melodies, accompanied by fortepiano*). Moscow: Tipografiia A. I. Mamontova, 1872, 56 pp., 2nd Ed., 1875, in Russian).

1. Vera Savvichna Mamontova,
by Valentin Serov, 1887

2. Sofia Fëdorovna Mamontova,
by Ilya Repin, 1879

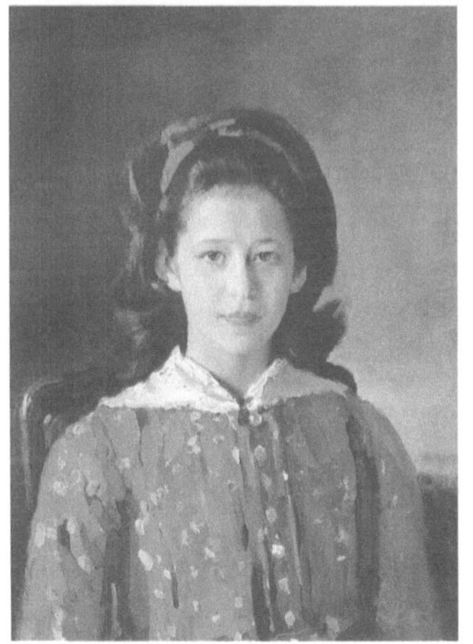

3. Liudmila Anatolyevna Mamontova,
by Valentin Serov, 1884

4. Tatyana Anatolyevna Mamontova,
by Ilya Repin, 1882

A back-translation of *Sonia*'s Mad Tea-Party fragment was published recently by Maria Isakova.[38] At the same time, the first

38 Isakova, Maria. "Russian 1879", in *Alice in a World of Wonderlands*, ed. J. Lindseth & A. Tannenbaum. Oak Knoll Press, 2015, Vol. 2. *Back*

5. *Ivan-Tsarevich na Serom Volke*, by Viktor Vasnetsov, 1889

detailed analysis was published (in Russian) of *Sonia*'s text, focusing on its comparison with several later translations.[39] The discussion of *Sonia*, as noted by Demurova, centres on the domestication attempts and the text's visible heterogeneity.[40] The book is abridged, but in an inconsistent way, with much difficult wordplay skipped. The book has ten chapters, not twelve; it is abridged but in an inconsistent way. Most of the Chapters I–VIII are translated almost verbatim, but then it seems that the trans-

Translations, pp. 171–173.

39 Ушакова, Т. А. "Mock nonsense: между Кэрроллом и русской сказкой (о первом переводе *Приключений Алисы в Стране чудес* на русский язык)". В кн.: Николаев, А. И., Николаев, И. и Ушакова, Т. А. *Тексты: слова и люди. Статьи и заметки по лингвокультурологии*. Иваново: ЛИСТОС, 2015, с. 115–130 (Ushakova, T. A. "Mock nonsense: mezhdu Kérrollom i russkoi skazkoi (o pervom perevode *Prikliuchenii Alisy v Strane chudes* na russkii iazyk)" / "Mock nonsense: between Carroll and the Russian fairy tale (on the first translation of *Alice's Adventures in Wonderland* into Russian)", in Nikolaev, A. I., Nikolaev, I., and Ushakova, T. A. *Teksty: slova i liudi. Stat'i i zametki po lingvokul'turologii* / *The Texts: the Words and the People. Papers and Notes in Linguoculturology*). Ivanovo: LISTOS, 2015, pp. 115–130 (in Russian).

40 Demurova, Nina M., "Sonja and Napoleon".

lator got exhausted and collapsed the remaining chapters, especially the ending. The text is intentionally heavily "Russified" (which sometimes happened with foreign fairy-tale translations in Russia) to make the book more comprehensible to children. However, a two-volume edition of the Brothers Grimm's *Folk-Tales* appeared in 1871 without any Russification; Andersen's and Hoffmann's tales have not been Russified. *Sonia*'s Russification is antiquated: the translator used archaic language, imitating the typical cadence of Russian folk fairy tales (available then from the collection by Afanasyev, published in 1858–1860). Some of the expressions used in *Sonia* were already out of date in the 1870s.

Ushakova discusses in detail the translator's decision on rendering the name of the Mock Turtle, probably the hardest of the *Wonderland* characters to recast in a foreign language.[41] She notes that a mock turtle soup was well-known in Russia at that time under its French name, *fausse tortu*; a reader (at least a middle-class one) would know that this dish was made from a calf's head. The French translators had no problem calling the character *Fausse Tortu*. Thus, based on Tenniel's illustrations, the *Sonia* translator rendered Mock Turtle simply as *Телячья Головка* (*Teliach'ia Golovka*, "a Calf-Head"). His (heavily abridged) final song says, "A wonderful calf-head soup!" This imagery was further developed into a nice pseudo-folkloric paragraph where the Calf-Head tells his sad story. Once upon a time, he was a real Calf (*телёнок, telënok*) among other calves, then someone decided to turn them into turtles—but apparently the metamorphosis was not completed. Accompanying the story are clever phonetic puns in a true Carrollian fashion: for example, the Calf-Head explains that all this happened in a saltwater pool (*солёный бассейн, solënyi basseyn*) but they called this pool a sea (*море, more*) because the calves were *morili* (*морили,* starved, tortured) there. A solution similar to "Calf-Head," but also based on Tenniel's illustrations, was independently used by Alexander Shcherbakov (1977), who called the Mock Turtle *Cherepakha-Teliach'i-Nozhki* (*Черепаха-Телячьи-Ножки,* 'a Calf-Feet Turtle'). For several new Evertype translations into rare languages, I advised rendering Mock Turtle

41 Ушакова, op. cit.

descriptively as a "Calf-Headed Turtle" (e.g., *Muzoobaş Taşbaka* in the first Kyrgyz translation by Aida Egemberdieva, 2016), following the *Sonia* tradition and Tenniel's illustrations.

In addition to *Sonia*'s text items discussed by Ushakova,[42] I would like to note a few other "markers". A very interesting decision by the *Sonia* translator is an added original Russian pun on the jurors. The translator cleverly noted that the word *присяжные* (*prisiazhnye* 'the jurors') invites a great, added phonetic pun (a Carrollian one-letter difference) with *пристяжные* (*pristiazhnye* 'side horses', that is, the two horses on the sides of the middle horse of a traditional Russian *troika*). Sonia confuses unfamiliar *prisiazhnye* with *pristiazhnye*, and then repeats the incorrect word *s samodovol'stviem* (*с самодовольствем* 'with a feeling of self-importance') several times, thinking that few girls of her age would know the meaning of this word. The translator's clear irony is that a trial by jury was then a great novelty in Russia: It was introduced by Alexander II in 1864, just a few years before *Sonia* was published. It would survive for only a half-century: The expression [*gospoda*] *prisiazhnye* [*zasedateli*] ([*господа*] *присяжные* [*заседатели*] 'gentlemen of the jury') was mocked as already outdated by a trickster hero, Ostap Bender (in Il'f & Petrov's *Двенадцать стульев / Dvenadtsat' stul'ev* ('*Twelve Chairs*'), 1928), ten years after the Bolsheviks did away with the fair judiciary system. For decades, trial by jury was so alien to Soviet language that Boris Zakhoder, in his accomplished *Wonderland* retelling (first published in a serialized magazine edition in 1971–1972), independently tried the same pun in reverse; his clever Alice *knows* the old-fashioned term for the jurors. Zakhoder tells his readers: "Do not confuse jurors (*prisiazhnye*) with side horses (*pristiazhnye*), and you will have as much reason to be proud of yourself as Alice. Even more: both are found these days much less often than a hundred years ago."[43] This Aesopian humor, unnoticed by censors, is very bitter: It was

42 Ibid.

43 Fet, Victor. "Beheading first: on Nabokov's translation of Lewis Carroll", in *The Nabokovian*, 2009, 63: 52–63.

during that time (the 1970s) that Soviet judges handed down sentences to political dissidents.

We can detect some Afanasyev fairy tale imagery in *Sonia* in a complex parody context. One of these clever, bizarre elements is the text that replaces "Father William." The Worm (i.e., the Caterpillar) orders Sonia to recite "*Blizko goroda Slavianska* …". This text is an aria from an extremely popular Russian opera, *Аскольдова могила* / *Askol'dova mogila* ("The Askold's Tomb") by Verstovsky (1835, libretto by Zagoskin), a song that had become very popular by 1879. Stylized as a medieval folk song, it tells about an evil nobleman who keeps a maiden in a deep cellar: "*iznyvala v zloy nevole / krasna devitsa dusha*" ("a good soul, a fair maiden suffered in the evil prison"). A very close phonetic parody delivered by Sonia is "*iznyvala v zlom rassole / belorybitsa dusha*" ("a good soul, a white fish, suffered in the spicy marinade"). This *belorybitsa* (*Stenodus leucichthys*, one of the largest fishes of the salmon family, then a common commercial fish of the Volga-Caspian basin), swam in from Russian legends and fairy tales. In the scary fairy tale *Сестрица Алёнушка и братец Иванушка* / *Sestritsa Alënushka i bratets Ivanushka* ('*Sister Alënushka and Brother Ivanushka*'), an enchanted girl wails to her brother from the bottom of the sea: "*liuta zmeia serdtse vysosala, belorybitsa ochi vyela*" ("the evil snake sucked out my heart, the white fish ate out my eyes"). Note a complete syllabic equivalence of *krasna devitsa* ~ *belorybitsa*, even with a matching color scheme *krasna* ~ *belo* ('red, fair' ~ 'white'). Such a freewheeling, multilayered parody would be expected from much later, twentieth-century nonsense writers such as Korney Chukovsky or even Daniil Kharms. It reminds one of *kapustniks* ("cabbage parties"), traditional gatherings of students or intellectuals, full of amateur songs, skits, spoofs, and parodies. One recalls Savva Mamontov's amateur theatricals that started exactly at this time (Christmas, 1878), and over a few years grew into the amazing Mamontov Private Opera.[44] The pseudo-medieval *Askold's Tomb* was by the 1870s a good old-fashioned target to parody. Other poetry in *Sonia* includes parodies of children reading from Zhukovsky (*Светлана*

44 Haldey, Olga, op. cit.

/ *Svetlana,* 1813), Pushkin (*Цыганы / Tsygany 'The Gypsies'*, 1824), and Mikhail Lermontov (*(Казачья колыбельная / Kazach'ia kolybel'naia 'The Cossack Lullaby'*), 1840), and a quote from Krylov (*(Квартет / Kvartet 'The Quartet'*), 1811). Some of these classical pieces would be independently utilized by later Russian translators.

The Duchess, who is not a playing-card character in *Wonderland*, becomes one in *Sonia*: *Пиковая Княгиня* (*Pikovaia Kniaginia*, "Princess of Spades"). The suit choice is a clever reference to Pushkin's novelette, *Пиковая дама / Pikovaia dama* (*The Queen of Spades*, 1834; Tchaikovsky's famous opera, based on this story, appeared later in 1890). Pushkin's old lady, in fact, was a Countess (*grafinia*), not a Princess (*kniaginia*). The suit assignment brings the Duchess into the deck, closer to her antagonist, the Queen of Hearts; the European Duchess (*Gertsoginia*, a title not found in Russia) is replaced by a Russian Princess. One of *Sonia*'s reviewers addressed the character as a *Queen* of Spades; the same error was made by Fan Parker; see reference on p. xi).

Russian translations always have a problem rendering the Queen of Hearts. The Russian deck has no Queens (*koroleva*); instead, it has Dames (*dama*), not an explicit royal rank. Usually, one disregards the correct playing-card terminology and uses a *Koroleva*. However, *Sonia*'s translator found a clever way out. The Queen is addressed as a *Краля* (*Kralia*), an old-fashioned term for a playing-card Queen; see, for example, Gogol's *Игроки / Igroki* ('*The Gamblers*', 1842). This regional word is derived from the Czech *král*, 'king', which has the same grammatical root as Russian *korol' / koroleva* ('king / queen'). Gogol' used *kralia* for a playing-card Queen already in his early stories about Ukraine (*Вечера на хуторе близ Диканьки / Vechera na khutore bliz Dikan'ki*) ('*Evenings on a Farm Near Dikanka*'), 1831). The word *kralia* still exists as an ironic slang word for a pretty woman, "a beauty", but the card term today is obsolete, and could not be used in a modern translation.

A very interesting domesticated parody in *Sonia* is the Mouse's "dry lecture". Demurova commented on the French Mouse arriving in Moscow with Napoleon.[45] It gives the Mouse's perspective of the French invasion of Russia in 1812. One has a feeling that, in 1879, this childish rendering slyly parodies not just a generic history book, but also the greatest Russian historical novel, read by nearly everyone at the time: *Война и мир / Voina i mir* ('*War and Peace*') by Lev Tolstoy (publ. 1868–1869). A careful analysis of *Sonja* might possibly reveal more interesting parallels; the text clearly was geared toward a middle-class child who would easily recognize the literary sources of the parodies. The book's high price (see reviews below) confirms that it was not intended for lower-class children.

A puzzling feature of *Sonia* is its complete anonymity; the book bears no indication of the author, the translator, or the illustrator. According to the censorship laws of the 1870s, a book manuscript could be presented to a censor without revealing the author's or translator's name. These would be requested only if a censor was suspicious of the content.[46] Just sixteen of Tenniel's illustrations were reproduced in *Sonia.* All of Tenniel's monograms and the Dalziels' signatures were carefully removed. Demurova says, incorrectly (p. xiii), that Tenniel's initials "were there at the bottom of every picture,"[47] but the copies in the Fales and St. Petersburg libraries both show that the initials were removed. Until now it has not been noticed that *Sonia* has *signature marks*—typographic features that identify leaves to ensure correct binding. They are located at the bottom-left side of nine pages (pp. 1, 17, 33, 49, 63, 81, 97, 129, and 161) and read Приключ. Сони (*Prikliuch. Soni*), an abbreviation of Приключения Сони (*Prikliucheniia Soni*, '*Sonia's Adventures*'). These signature marks preserved the important word "Adventures", which was not part of *Sonia*'s final title. This means that the Moscow publisher or the printer was aware of the original English title. Of course, in order to reproduce Tenniel's illustrations, a copy of *Wonderland* must have been available to Anatoly Mamontov in Moscow.

45 Demurova, Nina M., "Sonja and Napoleon".

46 Natalia Patrusheva, personal communication.

47 Demurova, Nina M., "Sonja and Napoleon".

When *Sonia* was recast into a Russified text, it was carefully purged of all English markers, down to replacing the price of the Hatter's hat with "50 kopecks." A similar replacement was done in the first Italian edition of 1872, and in a 1923 Russian translation by D'Aktil. This Russian price appears to be the cleverly calculated price of a *toy* hat, while Tenniel's iconic "10/6" in 1865 would be a *real* hat price.[48] The *Sonia* book itself was expensive, possibly due to the cost of illustrations: at 75 kopecks (0.75 ruble); it was correctly called "greatly overpriced" by one of the irate reviewers. At this time, an average worker's monthly salary was 20 to 30 rubles; a pound of meat was 20 kopecks.

The main remaining question is: Who was the translator? I'm reluctant to agree with the suggestions mentioned earlier that it was Olga Timiryazeva. I have found no evidence so far that she ever published any literary text or a translation. I would rather think that the Macmillan books were requested for the 23-year-old Ekaterina Timiryazeva (later Boratynskaya), who resided in St. Petersburg until February 1871. Twenty years later, she had developed into a fine, professional translator of English and American children's literature. It is possible that, by sending her the *Alice* translations, Lewis Carroll directly contributed to her early professional development and through that, indirectly, influenced generations of Russian children—including Boris Pasternak.

Sonia was published in Moscow eight years after Carroll's 1871 letter. Ekaterina Boratynskaya was then married and living in Moscow, which further strengthens her candidacy over Olga's. According to Ekaterina's memoirs,[49] she suffered nervous illnesses after her marriage and deaths in her family. She says that she fully recovered only by 1878—which would explain the seven-year gap between 1871 and 1878. *Sonia* could have been her first attempt in translation, experimenting with a hybrid folk style.

Sonia has an appearance of a work that was not properly finished and/or edited. Its last chapters are heavily truncated; many difficult pun sequences are left out; and some added expressions could represent traces of domestic charades that were

48 With a buying power of about £54, €64, or $67 as of 4 January 2017.

49 Лукьянов, С. М., op. cit.

not properly removed (see especially Notes 17, 33, and 42 below). It could be that the French and German translations of 1869 were requested with the aim of improving an early Russian draft that *already existed* (the Rev. Thompson could have possessed an English *Wonderland* copy as early as 1866 when Boratynskaya was 18 years old). However, by the time when Macmillan's books would have reached St. Petersburg, she already was married and moved to Moscow (January 1871). It is also possible that, due to her illness in 1871–1878, she did not finish her work on the manuscript, and it was eventually published without being completed. This could also explain its anonymity. There is also an added footnote in the book that probably does not belong to the translator (see Note 23).

Still, was Ekaterina Boratynskaya the translator of *Sonia*? Her later translations and abridged retellings were never Russified as *Sonia* was. All of her translations published in the 1890s would bear the author's name; at the same time, *Sonia*'s English identity was consciously concealed (although Tenniel's illustrations immediately give it up to anyone familiar with the original). Moreover, it would have been prudent for the translator to inform the author (or Macmillan, who sent her the *Alice* books, as we assume they did) that the translation had been published. However, it appears that no one ever told Carroll about the only Russian translation of *Alice* published in his lifetime.

At the same time, Maria Mamontova in Moscow was trying her hand at diverse educational and literary activities. Her productivity and networking were outstanding for a Russian woman of the 1870s.[50] Perhaps the Mamontovs commissioned *Sonia* independently. Anatoly Mamontov himself translated from German: He published a Russian translation of Goethe's *Faust* in 1897. Clearly, *Sonia* fits well among the early creative projects of the Mamontov circle.

I must note one more fascinating and possibly relevant connection. For thirty years after 1879, there would be no other

50 See e.g. my endnotes 8, 36, and 39, to pp. 19, 59, and 61 below, which point at some coincidences between the Mamontovs' publishing and performing in 1872–1882, and the folkloric references in the 1879 text of *Sonia*.

Russian translation of *Wonderland*, and then, within the short period of 1908 to 1913, four different translations appeared (by Matilda Granstrem, Alexandra Rozhdestvenskaya, Allegro, and an anonymous translation tentatively assigned to Mikhail Chekhov). Allegro (the 1909 translation) is the pen name of the poet Poliksena Solovyova (1867–1924), the youngest sister of the philosopher Vladimir Solovyov. Ekaterina Boratynskaya had been one of his close friends in the early 1870s. Is it a mere coincidence that 30 years later Poliksena Solovyova produced her own *Wonderland*? Vladimir Solovyov himself was a fine poet with a streak of parody and absurdism; in 1880, he translated *The Golden Pot* (*Der goldne Topf*) by E. T. A. Hoffmann; and in 1875 he traveled to London and met William Ralston Shedden-Ralston, the famous translator of Russian literature and fairytales (including Afanasyev), whom Lewis Carroll also knew.

There are several possible directions for further inquiry. The Russian archives might yield more information on Boratynskaya, the Timiryazevs, and the Mamontovs. *Sonia* might have been mentioned in the letters or diaries of the Mamontov or Solovyov children, or their friends and teachers. Finally, the text itself might contain more pointers, not dismissible as mere coincidences. Take, for example, the three "treacle well" girls whose names in *Sonia* are Dasha, Pasha, and Sasha. The names are quite common—but two of them are the same as the names of two of the Mamontov girls: Praskovya Anatolyevna ("Parasha" or "Pasha") is the daughter of *Sonia*'s publisher, and "Sasha" is Alexandra Savvichna, the youngest Mamontov baby, born in 1878. And, yes, "Sonia" was a common name at the time, as well—but it is also the name of Sofia Fëdorovna Mamontova, aged 13, painted by Repin in Abramtsevo, in a beautiful Russian dress, in the same year 1879 (see Fig. 2 above). It would be quite remarkable if *this* Sonia had *not* read *Sonia*!

I am grateful to many who answered my queries, including Alina Bodrova, Mark Burstein, Francesca Carlton-Jones, Mike S. Clark, Michael Everson, August A. Imholtz, Jr., Clare Imholtz, Sergey Kuriy, Jon Lindseth, Olga Luchkina, Chris Morgan, Eleonora Paston, Natalia Patrusheva, Abram Reitblat, Mark

Richards, Colin Salter, Byron W. Sewell, Elena Terkel′, Tatyana Ushakova, and Edward Wakeling.

Victor Fet
Huntington, West Virginia
February 2017

Рецензии на *Соню в царстве дива* (1879–1882)

Рецензии 1 и 2 найдены и перепечатаны А. М. Рушайло (1990, с. 93–95); рецензии 3 и 4 найдены и перепечатаны В. В. Лобановым (2000, с. 12–13) совместно с рецензиями 1 и 2 (Лобанов, 2000, с. 8–10). Текст воспроизводится согласно правилам современной орфографии.

(Без подписи). *Народная и детская библиотека*, М., 1879, № 3, с. 93–94.

***Соня в царстве дива*. Москва, 1879, 166 стран. Ц. 75 коп. С рисунками. Склад издания при магазине «Детское воспитание». Москва, Леонтьевский пер., дом Мамонтова.**

Уж и не издание ли это Мамонтовского магазина «Детское воспитание»? В маленькой книжке, переполненной орфографическими ошибками и стоящей непомерно дорого, помещён какой-то утомительно скучнейший, путанейший болезненный бред злосчастной девочки Сони; описание бреда лишено и тени художественности; остроумия и какого-либо веселья нет и признаков. Вот вам, читатели, на выдержку болезненные мозговые припадки Сони, очевидно страдающей горячечным бредом во сне: бежит кролик... кролик достал из кармана в жилете часы, взглянул на них и во все лопатки припустился бежать, Соня вскочила на ноги… Соня летела в глубокий колодец… по стенам колодца как будто шкафы, книжные полки; на гвоздях кое-где висят атласы, картины… Соня выпила из стакана – стала уменьшаться в росте… Соня плачет, слёзы собираются в лужу, и захватила лужа с *пол залы* (стр. 16-я, *правописание подлинника*)… Соня поскользнулась – и бултых, по горло окунулась в солёную воду (это из слёз-то! как это изящно)! В конце лужи мышь заплескалась... Лицо у ней (у мыши!) бледно как смерть… В лужу навалилися и утка, и журавль, и попугай, и орлёнок... Мышь говорит, что французы пошли на Москву, сразились под Бородиным… Птица, старая сорока, кутаясь в шаль, затрещала: «и мне, кажется, пора… Смеркается, горло боится простуды...». Соня пробралась в чистенькую комнатку, у окна стоит туалетный столик, на нём несколько пар новых перчаток и несколько вееров… Соня выпила из склянки, и всё растёт и растёт, ударилась головой о потолок… тесно становится… что делать? Оставалось одно последнее средство: одну руку высунуть в окошко, одну ногу просунуть в трубу (??)… Соня съела пирожок – росту убавилось… ходит Соня в лесу… щенок теребит прутик… Соня пустилась бежать со всех ног, как бы щенок не съел ее – она очень маленькая!.. Толстый синеватый черяк сидел на самой верхушке гриба и, сложив руки, спокойно курил предлинную трубку… Соня откусила гриба, и шея у нее вытянулась до макушек деревьев… шея сгибается и разгибается точно змеиная… Лакей-рыба подает письмо лакею-лягушке… Ребёнок – не ребёнок, а свинья… Сибирские кошки «скалятся»… Княгиня занялась ребёнком: споёт стишок (колыбельной песни) и тряхнёт ребёнка, «да так поддаст, что страшно глядеть»… Княгиня швырнула ребёнка прямо в Соню, а кухарка пустила в неё сковородой… За столом, Илюшка с зайцем сидят за чаем… карты: пятёрка, семёрка и т.д. играют на лугу в крокет… Из брони черепахи торчала телячья головка… На Соню налетела колода карт.

Довольно, читатель! Соня проснулась. Если промежутки между отрывками, выше приведёнными из книжки, наполнить всем содержанием, которое в ней заключается, смысла в книжке выйдет не более, чем в приведённых отрывках. Если б рассказ о Соне был даже переделкой откуда бы ни было – из Гофмана, из Эдгара По, вообще из причудливых фантазий поэта, мы и тогда сочли бы эту переделку неумелым, болезненным диким бредом. Можно и полезно увлекать иной раз детей *in das schöne Wunderland*—по Шиллеру, но это царство див, царство чудесного создаётся на известном чувстве *художественной меры*… Можно *поэтически* воспроизводить человеческие сны, но подобный мемориал патологического содержания о мозге, поражённом горячкой, что и представляет собою эта странная книжка о Соне, пригоден, быть может, для медицинских наблюдений и исследований, но никак не для забавного и художественно-воспитательного чтения детям.

(2) (Без подписи). *Воспитание и обучение*. СПб, 1879, № 10, с. 474–475.

***Соня в царстве дива*. Цена 75 к. Москва 1879.**

Издание опрятное на вид, со многими рисунками, не безобразными по исполнению и без опечаток, бумага хорошая – все эти достоинства мы признаём вполне, потому что масса покупает детские книги исключительно на основании таких достоинств; впрочем, надо оговориться, эта масса не принимает в соображение отсутствие опечаток и безобразие в рисунках, и для неё рисунки этой книжонки имеют недостаток, и весьма важный: они не расцвечены аляповато-яркими красками. Публика, которая ищет содержания в детских книжках, не найдёт его в «Соне в царстве дива». Царство дива – это нескладный сон девочки, который переносит её в мир мышей, кошек, белок, насекомых. Может быть, покупатель, перелистывая книгу, подумает, что найдёт в ней кое-какое подражание «Бабушкиным сказкам» Жорж Занд, и, разумеется, не рассчитывая найти ни крупного таланта, ни поэзии, будет всё-таки ожидать найти мысль – и ошибётся. Автор и не подозревает, что фабула его могла бы быть богатым источником, из которого дети почерпали бы поэзию мира природы, учились понимать влияние на человека, как в сказках Жорж Занд; он просто сплетает небылицу за небылицей, в которых нет никакого смысла, кроме грамматического, и преподносит всё это для услаждения досугов детей. Соня пьёт волшебные напитки, ест волшебные пироги и грибы, то вырастает, то становится крохотной под стать миру мышек, попадает в какой-то фантастический мир карт, – и нет конца нескладице. Положим, известно, что когда же сны бывали складны, но ведь сны, насмешившие нас нескладицей, рассказываются для смеха в своём кружке, а не печатаются на 166 страницах в 1/16 листа, не иллюстрируются и не преподносятся публике.

(3) «Е. С.» *Женское образование, педагогический листок для родителей, наставниц и наставников, издаваемый при Санкт-Петербургских женских гимназиях*. 1879, № 6–7 (Август–сентябрь), с. 469.

Соня в царстве дива. Москва, 1879 г., 166 стр. небольшого формата. Цена 75 коп.

Есть книги, о которых и десяти слов сказать не хочется, до того они «ниже критики». Лежащее перед нами издание принадлежит именно к их числу. Бессодержательнее и нелепее этой сказки, или, вернее, просто небывальщины (так как в создании *сказки* предполагается участие фантазии) трудно себе что-нибудь представить. Советуем всем матерям пройти мимо этого никуда не годного издания, не приостанавливаясь ни на минуту.

Е. С.

(4) Соболев, М. В. Обзор детских книг за 1879 г. *Педагогический сборник, издаваемый при главном управлении военно-учебных заведений.* СПб, 1882, вып. 2 (апрель–май–июнь), с. 287–337. (Рецензия на с. 297–298)

Соня в царстве дива. М. 166 с. мал. форм. Ц. 75 к.

В заграничной литературе существуют издания, в которых отношения и действующие лица изображаются в карикатурном виде и притом в степенях, увеличенных до последней возможности; при помощи таких сочинений надеются представить порок в отталкивающем виде и со слов других возбудить в детях отвращение к нему. Весьма сомнительна возможность достижения цели: осмеяние, позорное осуждение действует только на детей с развитым самолюбием, для других же выделяется комическая сторона: дети потешаются над недостатками, или, лучше сказать, над утрировкою их, не понимая хорошенько сущности того или другого ненормального явления.

В деле воспитания важнее развивать положительные стороны характера, чтобы в них человек находил опору для борьбы со всеми ненормальными явлениями.

Книжка «Соня в царстве дива» принадлежит к категории подобных изданий, хотя уступает заграничным в занимательности и талантливости. Русское сочинение скорее скучно, потому что с одной стороны мораль слишком выступает, а с другой похождения Сони малоинтересны. Восстаёт автор против *излишней любознательности*, страсти к разнообразным пожеланиям, пустой болтливости и т. д. Соня засыпает в саду и странствует в подземном пространстве, где она встречается и беседует с разнообразными животными, олицетворяющими этот или другой недостаток.

Превращения Сони в большинстве случаев бесцельны и сцены до крайности дики: напр., у Сони от выпитой жидкости до того разрастаются все члены, что одна нога вылезает в трубу, а рука за окошко, и только для того, чтобы ушибить кролика и вытолкнуть таракана. Как на одну из диких сцен, укажем на сцену в кухне пиковой дамы, в которую кухарка палит чем попало и чуть не убивает ребёнка.

Прочитав книжку, всё-таки кажется, что её писал человек, несколько знакомый с делом, именно превращения, которые испытывает Соня во сне, он приурочивает изменениям в положениях тела и внешним влияниям на сонного человека вообще. Если бы автор обладал более правильным и развитым воображением, то из темы вышла бы прекрасная сказка, теперь же ничего не получилось.

Reviews of *Sonia v tsarstvie diva* (1879–1882)

Reviews 1 and 2 were found and reprinted by A. M. Rushaylo;[51] reviews 3 and 4 were found and reprinted by V. V. Lobanov,[52] translated from Russian by Victor Fet.

The Russian spelling, grammar, and punctuation have changed considerably since the 1870s. In the orthographic reform of 1918, the Russian alphabet lost some letters, most notably the letter *ять* (*yat′,* ѣ), the letter i, and the terminal letter hard sign (ъ) was dropped. In this edition, spelling and grammar are modified to conform to the modern Russian norms.

1) Anon., In: *Народная и детская библиотека* (*Narodnaia i detskaia biblioteka / Popular and Children's Library*), Moscow, 1879, No. 3, pp. 93–94.

***Sonia v tsarstvie diva*. Moscow, 1879, 166 pp., price 75 kopecks, with illustrations. Publisher's warehouse at the "Children's**

51 Рушайло, А. М., op. cit.

52 Лобанов, В. В., op. cit.

Education" store, Moscow, Leontyevsky pereulok, Mamontov House.

Is this book also published by the Mamontov's "Children's Education" store? This little book, full of spelling errors and greatly overpriced, contains a kind of tiresome, extremely boring, confused, and morbid delirium of an ill-fated girl named Sonia; the description of this delirium lacks any shade of artistry; one finds no trace of wit or joy. Here are, for you the readers, some of Sonia's sickly brain attacks: here, a rabbit runs … the rabbit takes a watch out of its waistcoat-pocket, looks at it and then hurries on; Sonia now is up on her feet … Sonia falls into a deep well … there are cupboards and bookshelves on the sides of the well; here and there, maps and pictures hang upon nails … Sonia drinks from a bottle and shrinks … Sonia cries, her tears become a puddle, the puddle takes half of the room … Sonia slips—and falls up to her chin into saltwater (Made of her tears! How elegant!). There is a mouse in the end of the pool … Its face (the mouse has a face!) is pale as death … Now a duck and a crane fall into the same pool … A parrot, an eaglet … The mouse tells about the French coming to Moscow and fighting at Borodino … An old magpie with a shawl rattles: "I must be getting home … it is getting dark, my throat can get sore …" Sonia comes into a tidy little room with a small table, on the table there are several pairs of new gloves and several fans … Sonia drinks from a bottle, she grows and grows, her head hits the ceiling … it is getting too tight … what to do? the last resort was to put one arm out of the window, and one foot up the chimney (??) … Sonia eats a cake and shrinks again … Sonia walks in a wood … a puppy drags a stick … Sonia runs away, afraid that the puppy will eat her up—she is so small! … A fat blue worm sits on the top of a mushroom with folded hands and quietly smokes a very long pipe … Sonia bites off a piece of the mushroom, her neck stretches higher than trees … her neck bends and folds like a snake's … A fish footman gives a letter to a frog footman … A baby who is not a baby but a pig … Siberian cats are "grinning" … A Princess tends a baby: she sings a verse (of a lullaby) and shakes the baby "so hard it is scary to look" … The Princess tosses the baby right at Sonia; the cook throws a frying pan at her … At a table, Iliushka and a Hare are drinking tea … The cards (Five, Seven, etc.) play croquet on a meadow … A calf's head sticks out of a turtle's shell … A deck of card flies at Sonia.

Reader, enough! Sonia woke up. If one fills the gaps between the above-listed fragments from this book with all the omitted book's content, there still will be not much more sense than in those fragments. Even if the tale of Sonia were retold from any original source—from Hoffmann, from Edgar Poe, or any other elaborate fantasy of a poet—we still would consider this retelling to be unskilled, sick, and wild ravings. It is possible and useful sometimes to lead children, following Schiller, to *das schöne Wunderland*[53]—but such a realm of wonder, a realm of magic, would be based on a certain measure of *artistic balance*.… One can *poetically* reproduce human dreams—but such a memorial of pathological content of a delirium-stricken brain as this strange book about Sonia, though possibly useful for medical observations and studies, is in no way an entertaining and educational fictional reading for children.

2) Anon., In: *Воспитание и обучение*. (*Vospitanie i obuchenie / Upbringing and Education*), St. Petersburg, 1879, No. 10, pp. 474–475.

***Sonia v tsarstvie diva*. Price 75 kopecks. Moscow, 1879.**

This edition is accurate, with many illustrations that do not look ugly. It has no typing errors and is printed on good paper. We fully admit all this, since the masses buy children books exclusively based on those features; one must note that the masses do not care much for typing errors and ugly pictures; for them, however, illustrations of this book would lack a very important feature: a bright and gaudy coloring. Now, the public who look for content in

53 "*Nur ein Wunder kann dich tragen / In das schöne Wunderland*" ("Only wonder can bear thee / To the beautiful Wonderland") are the last lines in the 1801 poem "*Sehnsucht*" (Longing) by Friedrich von Schiller (1759–1805). It has been set to music many times, most notably by Schubert. (M. Burstein, *Knight Letter* 97.)

children books won't find it in *Sonia in a Kingdom of Wonder*. The Realm of Wonder is a scattered dream of a girl who is transported into a world of mice, cats, squirrels and insects. Possibly a buyer, leafing through this book, would hope to find in it some kind of imitation of Georges Sand's *Grandmother's Tales* and, certainly, not expecting to discover any great talent or poetry, would still try to find some thoughtfulness—and would be wrong. The author has no idea that his story could be a rich source from which children would absorb nature's poetry and learn to understand its influence on man, as in Georges Sand's tales; he just spins fantasy after fantasy, which make no sense, except a grammatical one, and presents this for consumption during a child's free time. Sonia drinks magic potions, eats magic cakes and mushrooms, grows and shrinks to the size of a mouse's world, finds herself in a fantastic world of playing-cards—and there is no end to this nonsense. Yes, it is true that dreams rarely make any sense—but dreams that are funny because of their nonsense are told and laughed at within a circle of friends, rather than being printed on 166 pages in 1/16 format, illustrated, and presented to the public.

3) E. S., In: *Женское образование* (*Zhenskoe obrazovanie / Women's Education*), 1879, No. 6-7, p. 469.

Sonia v tsarstvie diva. Moscow, 1879, small format, price 75 kopecks.

There are some books that are not worth a dozen words, so "beneath any critique" are they. The book that lies in front of us belongs exactly to such a class. It is hard to imagine anything that would make less sense than this fairy tale (or rather just a nonsensical story—since the creation of a fairy tale would at least require some fantasy). All mothers are advised to walk past this absolutely useless nonsense without stopping for a moment. – *E. S.*

4) Соболев, М. В. Обзор детских книг за 1879 г. *Педагогический сборник*. (Sobolev, M.V. Obzor detskikh knig za 1879 g. / A review of chidren books for 1879. In: *Pedagogicheskii sbornik / Pedagogical Collection*.) St. Petersburg, 1882, No. 2, pp. 287-337.

Sonia v tsarstvie diva. Moscow, 166 pp., small format, price 75 kopecks.

There are publications in foreign literature where the characters and their relationships are depicted as caricatures, exaggerated to an ultimate degree; those stories are designed to show vice in a disgusting way, and to impress children by showing how revolting it is. It is hardly doubtful that the aim could be achieved: Ridiculing and shaming can only affect those children who have a developed self-consciousness, while others would note only the comical side; children laugh at deficiencies or, rather, at the exaggeration of them, without a good understanding of abnormalities.

In children's education, it is important to develop the positive sides of a character, which would give a person a foundation for struggling against the abnormalities.

This book, *Sonia in a Kingdom of Wonder*, belongs to such kinds of publications, although it is less interesting and talented than the foreign ones. The Russian example is rather boring because, on one hand, the morality is overexaggerated, and on the other, Sonia's adventures are hardly interesting. The author objects to unnecessary curiosity, passions and wishes, empty talk, etc. Sonia falls asleep in a garden, and travels in the underground world, where she meets and talks with various animals that personify certain deficiencies.

Most of Sonia's transformations are pointless, and the scenes are wild: For example, Sonia drinks a liquid that makes all her limbs grow so large that one foot gets up the chimney, and an arm goes out the window—all this only in order to hit a rabbit and push out a cockroach. One of the wildest scenes takes place in the Queen of Spades' kitchen, where a cook throws all possible objects at the Queen and almost kills her baby.

It seems, upon reading this book, that the author was somewhat familiar with the subject: the transformations that Sonia experienced in her dream correspond to the changes in a body's position when asleep, and to general influences upon a sleeping person. If the author possessed a more organized and advanced imagination, this theme could produce a nice fairy tale; but nothing came out of this try.

Соня в царстве дива

Содержание

Глава I

У Кролика в норке

Скучно стало Соне сидеть без дела в саду около старшей сестры. Раза два она заглянула ей в книгу,—в книге ни картинок, ни разговоров. Какая радость в книге без картинок и разговоров!

День жаркий, душно. Соня совсем раскисла, её клонит ко сну; вздумала было плести венок, да надо встать, нарвать цветов. «Встать или не встать?» колеблется Соня, как вдруг, откуда ни возьмись, бежит мимо, близёхонько от неё, кролик—шкурка беленькая, глаза розовые.

Что Кролик пробежал—не диво; но Соня удивилась, что Кролик на бегу пробормотал про себя: «Батюшки, опоздаю!» Когда же Кролик достал из кармана в жилете часы, взглянул на них, и во все лопатки припустился бежать, Соня вскочила на ноги. Чтобы кролики ходили в жилетах, при часах!.. Нет, такой штуки она отроду не видывала и не слыхивала! Так разгорелось у Сони любопытство, что она бросилась за беленьким в погоню полем, и нагнала его как раз впору: Кролик только что шмыгнул в широкое отверстие норки около изгороди.

Соня туда же за ним.

Сначала дорога в норку шла прямая; потом вдруг обрывалась вниз, да так неожиданно и круто, что Соня не успела опомниться, как уже летела стремглав куда-то, словно в глубокой колодезь.

Взглянула вниз—зги не видать! Тогда Соня стала глядеть по сторонам. Видит—по стенам колодца как будто шкафы, книжные полки; на гвоздях кое-где висят атласы, картины.

Все ниже, ниже и ниже спускается Соня. «Когда же этому будет конец? Любопытно узнать, на сколько вёрст я уже провалилась! Эдак, пожалуй, я скоро окажусь где-нибудь около самого центра земли. Дай припомню: около 4000 вёрст, кажется, будет.» Соня, видите ли, уже знала кое-что из географии. «Ну, положим,» думает она, «я и спустилась на 4000 вёрст,[1] но под каким я градусом *широты* и *долготы*,—вот что всего важнее узнать.» Соня, надо заметить, не понимала хорошенько смысла широты и долготы, но слова эти сами по себе казались ей такими важными, славными, так тешили её.

«А что, если я провалюсь совсем, насквозь всей земли? Вот будет смех очутиться с людьми, которые ходят вверх ногами, на голове! *Антипатия*, кажется, это место называется…»[2] Тут Соня стала в тупик: с этим словом она не могла справиться, и обрадовалась, что некому было её подслушать. «Впрочем, о названии этой страны можно будет у них там справиться,» решила она, и стала представлять себе, как подойдёт к кому-нибудь, присядет и спросит: «Скажите, пожалуйста, что это—Новая Зеландия или Австралия?» Соня даже чуть не присела, но как тут присядешь на воздухе, летя вниз! «Впрочем, лучше не расспрашивать, а то, пожалуй, примут меня за невежду! Так и быть, не стану расспрашивать. Где-нибудь там у них да будет написано.»

Все ниже, ниже и ниже летит Соня. Что делать! Она опять принялась болтать. «Вот хватится меня Катюша! (Катюша у неё кошка.)[3] Надеюсь, её кто-нибудь попоит молоком за чаем. Катюша, милая! Хоть бы ты была здесь со мною! Мышей, правда, в воздухе не водится, ну, поймала бы себе летучую мышь; ведь простая мышь и летучая, я думаю, почти одно и то же? Не знаю только едят ли кошки летучих мышей?—вот что!..» Тут Соню стала разбирать дремота, и она то и дело повторяет: «Едят ли кошки летучих мышей? Едят ли мышей летучие кошки? Едят ли кошек летучие мыши?..» Соня дремлет, и кажется ей, будто она ходит рука об руку с Катюшей и строго допрашивает её: «Скажи, Катюшка, признайся, едала ты когда-нибудь летучую мышь? смотри, Катюшка, говори правду!..» Вдруг стук, стук, хлоп!—Соня свалилась на кучу сухих листьев и сучьев, и—стой, ни с места!..

Однако, она нисколько не ушиблась и тотчас вскочила на ноги. Взглянула вверх—темно; посмотрела вперёд—опять длинный ход, а по нему бежит, спешит Беленький Кролик. Не теряя минуты, Соня, как вихрь, понеслась за ним вслед, нагнала его на повороте, и слышит, говорит беленький: «Ай, ай, ай, как поздно!» Только Соня повернула за угол—глядит, а беленького и след простыл, словно провалился! Соня очутилась одна в длинной, низкой зале, сверху освещённой рядом ламп, которые висели с потолка.

По обеим стенам залы множество дверей: все заперты. Соня прошлась по всей зале, толкнулась в каждую дверь, ни одна не отпирается. Она отошла, и стала посреди залы. «Что мне теперь делать? Как выйти отсюда?» грустно думает она.

Соня обернулась и натолкнулась на столик. Столик этот о трёх ножках, весь из литого стекла. На нём лежит крохотный золотой ключик и больше ничего. «Этим ключиком, должно быть, отпирается хоть одна из всех этих дверей,» соображает Соня. Взяла ключик, пошла примерять его ко всем дверям—ни к одной не приходится,—как быть? Соня обошла залу ещё раз, и набрела на низенькую занавеску, которую сперва не заметила. Откинула занавеску—за нею дверка вершка[4] в 4 вышины. Она вложила ключ в замок—о радость!—ключ впору; отворила дверку, глядит: дверка выводит в коридорчик с мышиную норку; на самом конце коридорчика чудеснейший сад.

Соня стала на коленки, нагнулась, смотрит, и не налюбуется. Как бы она погуляла в этом саду, посидела около фонтана. «Но как быть? И головы не просунешь в узенькую дверку, а голову просунешь, плечи застрянут. Когда бы я могла вдвигаться и раздвигаться, как подзорная труба—вот было бы хорошо! Тогда я бы, кажется, справилась.»

Видя, однако, что нет пользы стоять у дверки, Соня воротилась к столику, не найдётся ли на нём другого ключика. На этот раз оказалась на столике скляночка с ярлыком. На ярлыке крупными, чёткими, печатными буквами была надпись: «ВЫПЕЙ МЕНЯ!»[5]

«Выпей меня,»—прочесть не мудрено; но взять, да так и выпить, не посмотреть, что пьёшь,—нет, не так глупа Соня! «Посмотрю сперва, не написано ли *наружное*,» рассудила она. Соня вспомнила, что когда на склянке написано *наружное*, то значит яд; и если выпить его слишком много, то может кончиться плохо.

На этой склянке, однако, не стояло *наружное*, и Соня решилась отведать. Отпила—ничего, вкусно; отзывается чем-то вроде всякой всячины; будто вишнёвым вареньем и яичницей, и ананасом, и жареной индейкой, и леденцом, и сдобными сухарями. Она допила всё до капельки.

«Что-то теперь будет? Престранное чувство!» говорит Соня. «Да никак я стала уменьшаться!..»

Так и есть: Соня действительно становится меньше да меньше. От неё осталось уже всего вершка четыре и как обрадовалась она, вздумав, что теперь она ростом как раз подходит к дверке, что выводит в чудесный сад! Постояла

Соня, подождала, не будет ли ещё чего, не вдвинется ли ещё? «Как бы совсем не вдвинуться!» струсила она. «Эдак, пожалуй, совсем исчезнешь, погаснешь как свечка,» говорит она самой себе.

Постояла Соня, видит, перемены нет, и решила, что тотчас отправится в сад. Пошла к дверке, а ключик от неё забыла на столике, воротилась к столику—что за горе! никак не достанет с него ключа, такая стала маленькая! Видит ключик сквозь стеклянный столик, а добраться до него не может. Что ни делала, как ни пробовала, ни хлопотала по ножкам взобраться на стол—ничего не поделаешь: скользко. Выбилась из сил бедная девочка, села и горько заплакала.

«Ну, разревелась!» вдруг спохватилась Соня. «Советую тебе сейчас перестать!» резко и строго унимает она себя. Соня, надо заметить, была вообще мастерица угощать себя не только советами, но иной раз даже и щелчками. Шли ли они ей впрок—другое дело. И теперь она было пустилась в разговоры с собою, но тотчас бросила, утерла слёзы и стала озираться на все стороны.

Вдруг, видит под стеклянным столиком лежит хрустальный ящичек. Она открывает его—в нём пирожок. На пирожке красиво выложены из коринки слова: «СЪЕШЬ МЕНЯ!» «Пожалуй, съем,» решила Соня. «Если выросту, достану ключ; а стану ещё меньше, пролезу под дверь. Что бы ни было,—лишь бы выбраться в сад.»

Соня откусила пирожка, съела кусочек, и страх её разбирает. «Что-то будет! Куда иду? Вверх или вниз?» Она подняла руки под головой, щупает вверх или вниз она уходит? Что за чудеса! Голова на месте, никуда не уходит! «Странное, однако, дело!» думает Соня. От пирогов, правда, никогда ничего не бывает особенного; но за это время с нею было столько диковинного, что её словно озадачило, и даже несколько обидело, что с нею не делается ничего особенного.

Она опять принялась за пирог и дочиста съела его.

Глава II

Слёзная лужа

«Чуднее и распречуднее,» закричала Соня. От удивления она даже путалась в словах, и выражалась как-то не по-русски. «Вот тебе раз! Выдвигаюсь теперь, как самая большущая подзорная труба! Стой, ноги, куда вы? Никак, надо проститься с вами!» И действительно, Соня, нагнувшись, едва уже видит ноги, так они вытянулись и далеко от неё ушли. «Ну уж теперь никак не достану обувать их,» рассудила она и вдруг стукнулась головой о потолок—она вытянулась чуть не на сажень. Она проворно схватила со стола ключик и поскорей к садовой дверке. Бедная Соня, опять неудача!—В дверь не пройдёт. Только растянувшись во всю длину, она могла приложиться к ней одним глазом и заглянуть в сад; но пройти—куда при таком росте! не выдержала тут Соня, опять расплакалась.

«Постыдилась бы себя, коли других не стыдно! Такая большая, да плачет» (и подлинно большая!) «Ну, будет, сейчас перестань, слышишь!» Ни увещания, ни угрозы, ничего не помогает; Соня плачет, рыдает, разливается; в три ручья текут у неё слёзы, собираются в порядочно глубокую лужу, и захватила эта лужа уже с ползалы.

«Уж не заколдовал ли меня ночью колдун, или волшебница?» подумала Соня. «Дай вспомню, было ли со мною что-нибудь особенное нынче утром? Да, будто что-то было не как всегда. Ну, положим, я стала не Соней, а кем-то другим, так куда же девалась я, настоящая Соня, и в кого я обернулась?»

Соня стала перебирать всех ей знакомых девочек, не узнает ли, в которую именно она обернулась. «Уж не стала ли я Аней?—Нет, не может быть: у Ани волосы длиннее моих и вьются, а мои совсем не вьются. И Машей я не стала—я учусь хорошо, и уже много знаю, а Маша учится дурно и ничего не знает. Однако с моей головой как будто что-то неладное делается!.. Попробовать разве припомнить, знаю ли я впрямь всё, что знала. Ну-ка: 4 × 5 = … 12; 4 × 6 = … 13; 4 × 7 = … Сколько бишь?… эдак, пожалуй, и до 20-ти не досчитаешь…. Ну, да что таблица умножения—это неважно! Посмотрим, как из географии: Лондон—столица… Парижа, а Париж?.. —столица Рима, а Рим?.. Ну, поздравляю, всё вздор!.. И вправду не обернулась ли я в Машу.

Попробую, как со стихами. Ну-ка: „*Птичка Божия не знает*“!» Соня сложила перед собою руки, как привыкла за уроком, и начала. Голос её в этой пустой зале казался глухим, хриплым, будто не своим, а слова все выходили навыворот, и никак она не сладит с языком:

«Киска хитрая не знает
Ни заботы, ни труда:
Без хлопот она съедает
Длиннохвостого зверька.
Долгу ночь по саду бродит,
Как бы птичку подцепить,
И, мурлыча, песнь заводит,
Чтоб доверье ей внушить.
А как утром солнце встанет,
Люди выйдут погулять,
Киска сытенькая сядет
Морду лапкой умывать.[6]

И всё не так, всё по-дурацки!» говорит бедная Соня, и так ей досадно, чуть не до слёз. «И выходит, что я обернулась в Машу—это так верно, как нельзя вернее!.. Не хочу я быть Машей! Ни за что, ни за что!.. Господи, да что же это такое!» вдруг разрыдалась Соня, «хоть бы кто-нибудь просунул сюда голову! Уж мне так скучно сидеть здесь одной!..»

Соня опустила голову и, нечаянно взглянув себе на руки, видит, что в жару разговора с собою она и не заметила, что она словно тает. Соня вскочила, пошла к столику помериться. И то,—уж немного от неё осталось. «Хорошо сделала, что выбралась из воды,» думает Соня, «а то бы, пожалуй и совсем растаяла!» «Теперь в сад!» закричала она и со всех ног бросилась к двери. Час от часу не легче!—

Дверь опять заперта, а золотой ключик опять лежит на стеклянном столике.

«Это уж просто из рук вон! Где же мне такой крошечной достать его! Уж это так худо, что хуже и нельзя; терпения моего не стало—вот что!» и с этими словами Соня поскользнулась—и бултых, по горло окунулась в солёную воду.

«Потону ещё, чего доброго, в собственных своих слезах, и будет это мне наказанием, чтобы я вперёд не плакала, как дура.» Вдруг, на том конце лужи заплескалось что-то. Соня подплыла разузнать, что такое. Она было струсила, но потом успокоилась и подумала на мышь.

«Точно—мышь. Не заговорить ли мне с нею,» думает Соня. «Здесь всё так удивительно, что и мыши, пожалуй, говорят; я этому нисколько бы не удивилась. Попробовать разве?—Спрос не беда. Мышь, мышка! Скажите, пожалуйста, как мне выбраться из этой лужи? Я совсем измучилась, плавая в ней, да и растаять боюсь!» Мышь с любопытством обратилась острыми глазками на Соню, прищурилась, но ничего не отвечала.

«Она, может быть, не понимает по-русски,» думает Соня. «Может быть, это мышь французская, пришла в Россию с Наполеоном. Посмотрим, скажу что-нибудь по-французски.» Первое, что ей вспомнилось из французских уроков, она и сказала: «Où est ma chatte?» Как прыгнет Мышь одним скачком вон из лужи, стоит, вся трясётся. Соня догадалась, хоть и поздно, что сильно напугала её. «Ах, простите меня, пожалуйста!» поспешила она извиниться, «я совсем забыла, что вы не любите кошек.»

«Не люблю!» сердито и резко завизжала Мышь, «посмотрела бы я, как ты на моём месте стала бы целоваться с кошкой.»

«Уж, конечно, не стала бы,» вкрадчиво говорит Соня, желая помириться с Мышью. «Только, пожалуйста, не сердитесь. Но знаете ли, если бы вы хоть раз взглянули на нашу кошечку Катюшу, наверное полюбили бы её. Уж такая наша Катюша ласковая, такая милашка!» болтаясь в луже, припоминает Соня, совсем забыв про Мышь. «Уж такая эта Катюша у нас драгоценный зверёк: сидит около печки, курлычит, лапки себе лижет, мордочку умывает! И такая она чистенькая, мягонькая, тёпленькая! С рук бы не спустила. А какая мастерица ловить мышей… Ах, что же это я опять!.. пожалуйста, простите!» спохватилась вдруг Соня, взглянув на Мышь.

А эта стоит натопорщенная. «Ну, теперь уж непременно обиделась,» думает Соня. «Лучше нам вовсе об этом не говорить,» успокаивает она Мышь.

«*Нам!!!*» закричала Мышь, а сама трясётся с головы до самого кончика хвоста. «Стану я говорить о такой гадости! В нашем семействе всегда ненавидели кошек. Гадкий, низкий, подлый зверь—вот что! И чтобы уши мои не слышали, глаза мои не видали!.. Прошу покорно меня этим не угощать.»

«Не буду, не буду. Давайте разговаривать о другом,» предлагает Соня, стараясь придумать, чем бы развлечь Мышь. «Скажите, какое ваше мнение о собаках? Любите ли вы собак?» На это Мышь ни гу-гу. Соня обрадовалась. «Есть у нас, знаете, около дома, премиленькая собачка,» начинает Соня. «Вот уж понравилась бы вам! Глазки у неё быстрые, острые; шубка тёмная, кудрявая и уж каких-каких штук она не знает! Хозяин её, наш староста,[7] не нахвалится Жучкой. Такая, говорит, смышлёная, полезная, за сто рублей не отдать. В амбарах у него всех крыс, да мы…. Ах, батюшки, что же это я опять!» остановилась Соня. И жалко, и совестно ей. «Ах, какая досада, опять я вас нечаянно обидела!» Соня оглянулась на Мышь, видит—удирает от неё Мышь, что есть мочи и такую подняла плескотню в луже, что страсть!

Тогда Соня тихим, мягким голосом стала её к себе звать. «Мышка, душенька, пожалуйста, вернитесь! Право не стану больше говорить о кошках и собаках—вижу теперь, как они вам противны.» Мышь, на эти слова, тихо стала подплывать к Соне. Лицо у неё было бледно, как смерть (верно, со злости, подумала Соня); и говорит Мышь дрожащим голосом: «Выйдем на берег; там я расскажу тебе повесть моей жизни, и ты поймёшь тогда, почему я ненавижу кошек и собак.»

И пора было выбираться из лужи: в ней становилось тесно. В неё навалилась бездна всякого народа: были тут и Утка, и Журавль, и Попугай, и Орлёнок, и кого только не было![8] Соня поплыла вперёд, все за нею, и целой партией выбрались на берег.

Глава III

Игра в горелки[9]

Престранное собралось общество на берегу. Птицы все растрёпанные, хохлы взъерошенные, перья болтаются по бокам; звери прилизанные, шубки мокрые насквозь, с них льёт, течёт, и все они, нахохленные, надутые, глядят сентябрём.[10]

Первым делом надо было обсушиться. Стали об этом держать совет; Соня тут же с ними толкует, рассуждает, нимало не конфузясь, точно век знакома с ними. Она даже пустилась с Попугаем в спор, но он скоро надулся и зарядил одно: «Я старше тебя, стало быть, и умнее тебя.» А насколько старше, не хочет сказать. Так Соня видит, что ничего от него не добьёшься и замолчала.

Тогда Мышь вступилась. Она, как видно, была между ними важное лицо. «Садитесь и слушайте,» сказала она, «вы у меня скоро обсохнете.» Все расселись в кружок, Мышь посерёдке. Соня жадно уставилась на неё. «Что-то она скажет,» думает она, «поскорее бы обсохнуть, а то так холодно,—ещё простудишься, пожалуй!»

«Ну-с,» с достоинством начала Мышь, «все ли на месте? Сухо же здесь, нечего сказать! Прошу покорнейше всех молчать. Было это в 12-м году. Мы с Наполеоном шли на Россию, хотели брать Москву. Я ехала в фургоне с провиантом, где ни в чём не нуждалась и имела очень удобное помещение в ранце одного французского солдата.» Тут Мышь важно приподняла голову и значительно оглянула всё общество. «Полководцы у нас были отличные, привыкли воевать: куда ни пошлют их, везде побеждают. Пошли на Москву, сразились под Бородиным...»

«Б-р-р-р,» затрясся Попугай—очень его уж пробирало.

«Вам что угодно? Вы, кажется, что-то сказали?» учтиво обратилась к нему Мышь, а сама нахмурилась и сердито водит усами.

«Ничего-с, я так только,» поспешил отвечать Попугай.

«Мне, стало быть, почудилось,» отрезала Мышь. «Так, дальше, продолжаю. Сразились под Бородиным, одержали победу, вступили в Москву зимовать. Всё бы хорошо, не случись беды. Москва стала гореть, а кто поджёг, неизвестно. Русские говорят на французов, французы сваливают на русских—кто их разберёт. Я в то время жила во дворце и была свидетельницей всего, что происходило.»[11] И Мышь опять значительно оглянула общество. «Ну, видит Наполеон, что плохо дело, собрал совет, много толковали и нашли… Ну что, душенька, обсохла?» вдруг обратилась Мышь к Соне.

«Нисколько, мокрёхонька, как была,» пригорюнившись, отвечает Соня.

«Господа,» торжественно выступил тут Журавль, «имею предложить заседанию распуститься для принятия более энергических мер…»

«Говори по-русски,» закричал на него Орлёнок, «из твоих мудрёных слов я ничего не пойму, да и сам ты, чай, их, брат, в толк не возьмёшь.» И Орлёнок засмеялся исподтишка; но это заметили другие птицы и поднялось хихиканье.

«Я хотел только, в виду общего блага, предложить игру в горелки; а впрочем, как будет угодно,» несколько обиженно сказал Журавль.

«Что же это за игра?» спросила Соня и только потому, что ей стало жалко Журавля, который после выходки Орлёнка стоял сконфуженный.

«Чем пускаться в объяснения, лучше показать на деле,» отвечал Журавль и вышел на середину.

Он расставил всех по парам и не успел стать в свою пару, как пошла беготня без толку. Все побежали разом. Толкотня, путаница, и никто не разберёт, кому гореть, кого ловить. Потолкавшись так с полчаса, они-таки порядочно пообсохли; вдруг Журавль скомандовал: «Стой, господа, игра кончена!» Запыхавшись, все обступили его.

Соне стало жарко, она хочет достать платок, опускает руку в карман и в нём оказывается коробочка с леденцами, к счастью, не промокшая в воде. Соня вынула коробочку и принялась угощать всю компанию.

Принялись за леденцы, но и тут неудача. Поднялся шум, гвалт. Длинноносые, крупные птицы не справятся с леденцом, не знают, как пропустить его в клюв. Мелкие давятся им,—пришлось колотить их по спине, чтобы проскочить. Наконец, кое-как справились, успокоились и, рассевшись опять в кружок, попросили Мышь рассказать что-нибудь.

«Вы обещались рассказать про себя, помните,» обратилась к ней Соня. «Хотели рассказать, почему вы ненавидите К... и С...» шёпотом добавила она, боясь опять раздразнить её.

«Ах, грустная и длинная повесть моей жизни,» вздохнула Мышь, глядя на Соню.

«Длинная-то, длинная!» подумала Соня, оглядываясь на мышиный хвост, «но почему грустная, любопытно знать,» продолжала она про себя. Очень смущал её этот длинный хвост, не оторвать от него глаз и мысли. Мышь рассказывает, а Соне чудится, что рассказ её извивается вниз по хвосту, как по дорожке, в следующем виде:—

«Однажды
Громи-
ло,[12] дво-
ровый
злой
пёс,
наско-
чил на
мышь;
без суда,
без рас-
правы
к суду
пота-
щил:
„Бла-
го дела
мне
нет,“
гово-
рит
он,
зло-
дей:
„без
суда и
судей
при-
сужу
тебя
к смер-
ти.“»

«Ты, кажется, не слушаешь?» строго вдруг покосилась Мышь на Соню. «О чём ты думаешь и куда глядишь?»

«Извините, пожалуйста,» поспешила оправдаться сконфуженная Соня. «Я всё слышала; вы, кажется, остановились на пятом повороте.»

«Ворона!» яростно взвизгнула Мышь.

«Где, где! Дайте, я поймаю» бросилась Соня, не понимая, в чём дело.

«Какие тут вороны!» ещё более взбесилась Мышь, собираясь уходить. «Вы оскорбляете меня вашими глупыми речами!»

«Право, я не нарочно… Я думала… Мне показалось… Да что же это вы беспрестанно обижаетесь!» взмолилась Соня.

Мышь только фыркнула в ответ.

«Пожалуйста, воротитесь, расскажите дальше,» упрашивала Соня.

«Пожалуйста, воротитесь, расскажите дальше,» повторили все за нею хором. Но Мышь не внимала; мотнула только головой, и ещё чаще засеменила ножками.

«Жаль, что ушла,» заметил Попугай, глядя уходящей Мыши вслед. «Ну, характер!» обратилась жирная старая Жаба к молодой. «Видишь, как нехорошо злиться! пусть тебе это будст наукой…»

«Уж, пожалуйста, отстаньте!» с сердцем прервала молодая Жаба, «вас слушать терпения не хватит. Устрица на что дура, и та не выдержит—лопнет.»

«Была бы Катюшка здесь со мною, сейчас воротила бы Мышь,» сказала Соня вслух, но не обращаясь ни к кому особенно.

«А кто такая Катюшка, позвольте узнать?» спросил Попугай.

«Это у нас такая кошечка Катюша,» живо начинает Соня. Она радёхонька случаю поговорить о своей любимице. «Да какая ловкая мышей ловить! А посмотрели бы вы как она за птицами! только увидит и цап-царап—съела. Уж такая мастерица!»

Едва Соня это сказала, переполошились птицы. Некоторые поспешно разлетелись. «И мне, кажется, пора,» затрещала старая Сорока, кутаясь в шаль; «уже смеркается, а у меня горло ужасно боится сырости. Совсем голос пропадет!» «Домой, домой, спать пора!» зазвенела дрожащим голосом Канарейка, сзывая своих птенцов. Так, понемногу разошлись все и Соня опять осталась одна.

«Лучше бы мне вовсе не поминать о Катюше,» пригорюнившись, сказала она. «Никому-то она здесь не мила, а ведь лучше моей Катюши на свете нет! Милая, дорогая, золотая моя Катюшечка! Когда-то мы с тобою свидимся! Ну как никогда!..» Не выдержала Соня, разрыдалась: так скучно и горько стало ей здесь одной. Вдруг слышит, опять топочат чьи-то маленькие ножки. Оглянулась, не Мышь ли одумалась, идёт назад досказывать длинную повесть свой жизни?

Глава IV

Кролик посылает Ваську на врага

Не Мышь, а Беленький Кролик топочет, идёт не спеша, озирается по сторонам, будто что ищет, и походя ворчит: «Пропали мы с вами, ножки мои золотые; пропали, матушка шубка, сударики усики! Загубит, казнить велит Червонная Краля!..[13] Да куда это они, злодейки, запропастились?..»

Вскоре заметил Кролик Соню и сердито закричал: «Матрёна Ивановна, а Матрёна Ивановна![14] Сбегайте-ка скорей домой, принесите перчатки, да веер; да проворнее, проворнее же, говорят вам!» Соня с испуга ударилась бежать, куда указывал Кролик.

«Пусть думает Кролик, что я Матрёна Ивановна; это у него, должно быть, кухарка,» рассуждает она сама с собою. «Вот удивится, как узнает, что я не Матрёна Ивановна!» Прибежала Соня, видит: стоит маленький хорошенький домик; на двери прибита медная дощечка; на дощечке написано: «ДОМ ЦЕРЕМОНИЙМЕЙСТЕРА КРОЛИКОВ-

СКОГО.»[15] Соня, не постучавшись, отворяет дверь, вбегает на лестницу, спешит отыскать перчатки, веер, сама боится, не встретить бы ей эту Матрёну Ивановну,—не выгнала бы она её из дому.

«Странно, однако, быть на побегушках у кролика?» думает Соня. «Эдак, пожалуй, и Катюшка вздумает меня гонять!!!»

Между тем она пробралась в чистенькую, маленькую комнатку: у окна стоит туалетный столик; на нём несколько пар новых перчаток и несколько вееров. Она проворно берёт с него пару перчаток, веер и собирается выходить, как вдруг, взглянув ещё раз на туалетный столик, видит, у зеркала стоит склянка, на ней нет ярлыка с надписью: «ВЫПЕЙ МЕНЯ», но Соня думает, не мешало бы отпить от неё. Откупорила, отпила, «чего я здесь ни поем и ни напьюсь, всегда выходит что-нибудь да необыкновенное,» рассуждает Соня; «посмотрим, что из этого выйдет—хоть бы мне вырасти! А то право, очень уж надоело быть такой крохотной!..»

Не успела Соня пожелать, глядь, она уже подымается, растёт выше, выше, да так быстро, что в один миг ударилась головой о потолок и только успела нагнуться, чтобы не свернуть шеи. «Будет, больше не стану пить,» сказала Соня и бросила склянку. «Ну, опять беда,—не вылезу теперь из двери; напрасно я столько отпила!»

Поздно было об этом жалеть: Соня всё растёт да растёт; спустилась на колени—мало, тесно становится; свернулась, съёжилась: одним локтем упёрлась в дверь, другую руку занесла на голову,—всё мало: растёт, да растёт. Что делать? оставалось одно, последнее средство: одну руку высунуть в окошко, одну ногу просунуть в трубу.

Просунула и думает Соня: «Кончено, теперь уж ничего не поделаешь. Что-то со мною будет!»

Тут Соня, к радости своей, заметила, что больше не растёт. И то хорошо, но как бы то ни было, положение её было крайне неприятное и неловкое. Каким образом избавиться от него, ума не приложишь! Соня приуныла.

Долго ли, нет ли лежала Соня, только вдруг слышит она издали чей-то голос; прислушивается: «Матрёна Ивановна, а Матрёна Ивановна, куда вы пропали? что не несёте перчатки?», затем, топы, топы, взбирается кто-то по ступенькам на лестницу. Как заслышала Соня голос да шаги Кролика, вся затряслась, даже весь дом покачнулся. И чего она, глупенькая, испугалась! чуть не забыла, что при её росте не страшен ей ни Кролик, ни всякий другой зверь.

Подошёл Кролик к двери, хочет отпереть—не подаётся: дверь отпирается внутрь, а Соня локтем припёрла её. Не сладил Кролик, отошёл и слышит Соня: «Ну,» говорит, «влезу в окно.»

«Как же, непременно, попробуй-ка,» подсмеялась Соня. Заслыша Кролика под окном, она вдруг как растопырит пальцы... (Руку-то одну она ведь высунула в окно.) Слышит, писк, хлоп! задребезжали стёкла где-то внизу, будто провалился кто в рамы парника.

Затем яростный крик Кролика: «Петька, Петька, где ты, бездельник?»[16] Отвечает ему чей-то незнакомый голос, словно петуший: «Здесь я, в навозной куче, спаржу рою вашей милости.»

«Роет спаржу!» с сердцем кричит Кролик. «Иди сейчас, вытащи меня отсюда!» И опять хруст, лязг побитых стёкол.

«Гляди-ка Петька, что это там торчит в окне»

«Никак рука, ваша милость.»

«Рука, хохлатый тетерев![17] когда ж бывают такие руки! эта ручища, не видишь, что ли, загородила всё окно!»

«Загородила-то, загородила, а всё ж это рука, ваша милость!»

«Ну, пусть, ручища, только ей там незачем быть, и ты у меня сейчас пойди, чтобы не было её!»

Молчание. Изредка только, слышит Соня, перешёптываются под окном. «Воля ваша, сударь, не пойду: больно страшно.» «Трусишка, смеешь ты ослушиваться! делай, что тебе приказывают, не то!..» Тут Соня опять растопырила пальцы. На этот раз запищали в оба голоса, потом хлоп, хлоп! и опять задребезжали стёкла. «Сколько же у них там должно быть парников!» подумала Соня. «Что-то они теперь станут делать! Хоть бы догадались вытащить меня в окно; сил моих нет скорчившись лежать.»

Ждёт Соня, прислушивается—ничего не слыхать. Спустя немного, слышит, катится что-то, будто везут телегу; говор на разные голоса. «Лестницу, ребята! тащите лестницу,» говорит один. «Эй, Петька, тащи её сюда, на угол станови!»

«Эх, коротка, братцы,» кричит другой; «одной мало, другую подавай! Верёвкой её связать!»

«Эй, Васька, верёвку хватай, связывай!»[18]

Приставили лестницу, взбирается кто-то, вдруг стал: «И крепка ли крыша, ребята,» говорит, «вот что, не провалиться бы!»

«И то! Глядит-ка, гляди, никак доска ползёт! Берегись, ребята, головы прочь!»; кто-то хлопнулся о землю, и пошёл треск и гром внизу.

«Эй, братцы, никак Петька слетел? и то, слетел.»

«Кому ж теперь, братцы, в трубу-то лезть?»

«Как знаете, я не полезу.»

«Ты, Васька, полезай!»

«Ишь, ловкий! не пойду, сам полезай!»

«Кому, сударь, прикажете лезть?»

«Ваське,» приказал Кролик.

«Васька, барин тебе велит!»

Соня просунула ногу в трубу, сколько можно было выше, и ждёт; слышит, в трубе поднялась возня; скребёт, шаркает что-то близёхонько над ней.

«Ну, Васька идёт,» думает она и что есть мочи брыкнула в него ногой. Ждёт. Вот, слышит; загомонили внизу на все голоса: «Во-на! Васька, Васька-то вылетел!» Потом Кролик вопит: «Вон, вон он, около изгороди лежит!», всё затихло на время, потом опять заголосили; слышно, будто хлопочут около Васьки.

Один кричит: «Голову держи! Водкой отпоить!»

«Да тише вы, братцы,» кричит другой; «помаленьку, не то захлебнётся! Ну, что, брат Васька, отлегло ли?»

«Говори, что, как было?» говорит Кролик. «Как это тебя из трубы выкинуло?»

Тут запищал кто-то слабеньким голосом.

«Это Васька очнулся,» решила Соня.

«И не припомню, братцы, что тут было: как поддало из трубы, индо в глазах помутилось!.. Я в трубу, а из трубы как пырнёт в меня чем-то,—я, братцы, и не взвидел света. Вылетел словно пуля!..»

«Что и говорить, важно вылетел!» поддакнули все. Опять замолчали.

«Поджечь разве дом?» спустя немного, вдруг говорит Кролик. «Попробуйте-ка, дураки!» закричала тут Соня во весь голос. «Вот погодите, натравлю я на вас Катюшку!»

Всё смолкло. «Ну,» думает Соня, «что-то они теперь затеют! Хоть бы догадались крышу разобрать.» Немного погодя, опять голос Кролика: «И одного будет воза для начала.»

«Чего это, одного воза?» думает Соня. Скоро узнала чего, как посыпалась на неё куча камушков, и ударились ей прямо в лицо. «Забьют теперь, пожалуй, коли их не унять! Ну, вы там, полноте, дурачьё!» Опять всё замолкло, не слыхать ничего.

Вдруг Соня видит: брошенные камушки превращаются в пирожки. «Что за диво! Попробовать разве съесть хоть один,» пришло ей на ум. «Какая-нибудь да выйдет перемена! Вырасти ещё больше не вырасту—это верно; а стану меньше,—тем лучше.»

Соня взяла пирожок,—съела; замечает, точно, росту несколько убавилось. То-то обрадовалась! Выждала покуда не поравнялась с дверью, отперла её и выбежала из дому. Около двери толпилась куча всяких зверят и птиц: тут был и Петька-петух, и черномазый Васька-таракан. Его держали двое поросят и чем-то отпаивали. Увидя Соню, они было кинулись на неё, но она бросилась от них бежать и вскоре очутилась в дремучем лесу.

Ходит Соня по лесу, как вдруг над самой головой её раздаётся резкий, визгливый лай. Озадаченная Соня проворно подымает голову, видит—огромный щенок таращится на неё круглыми, глупыми глазами и тянется ударить её лапой. «Щеночек, голубчик,» подзывает его Соня, даже свистнула, а сама до смерти трусит, не проголодался ли щенок: она такая маленькая, не вздумал бы её съесть.

Растерялась Соня, не знает как быть; подняла прутик, бросила его щенку. Как подпрыгнул щенок четырьмя лапками вверх, да кинется вперёд за прутиком, а Соня проворно шмыг от него за кусты, и выглядывает оттуда,—

уж очень она испугалась. А щенок теребит прутик, скачет, мечется, ворчит, лает, визжит. Соня ни жива, ни мертва. Наконец щенок, видно, измучился, запыхался совсем; уселся, передними лапами врозь, высунул красный, широкий язык и щурит глупые глазёнки.

Соня решилась воспользоваться этим временем, и со всех ног пустилась бежать. Далеко убежала, еле опомнилась!

«А какой миленький был щеночек!» размышляет Соня, едва переводя дух, опершись на цветок и обмахиваясь листком. «Была бы я настоящего роста, каким бы славным штукам я его выучила! Ах, да что же это, я чуть не забыла.

Ведь мне нужно вырасти; подумаю, как это делать: уж не съесть ли или выпить чего-нибудь?»

Соня пошла, глядит по сторонам; то подойдёт к цветку, осмотрит листья, то заглянет в траву,—нет ничего и похожего, что бы можно было съесть. Идёт дальше, видит перед нею сидит гриб, как раз с неё ростом; она обошла кругом гриба, внимательно осмотрела его, заглянула ему под шапочку, поднялась на цыпочки, вытянула шею, подняла голову и встретилась глазами с большим, толстым, синеватым червяком. Он сидел на самой макушке гриба, и, сложив руки, спокойно курил предлинную трубку.

Глава V

Советник-Червяк

Глядит Червяк на Соню, Соня на Червяка. Поглядели они так молча друг на друга. Вынул, наконец, Червяк трубку изо рта, и говорит Соне, да таким сонным голосом, едва тянет:

«Кто ты такая?»

Этот вопрос очень озадачил Соню; она никак не ожидала, что этим начнётся у них разговор, и, несколько сконфуженная, говорит Червяку: «Право, сударь, я и сама не знаю. Нынче утром, вставши, я знала, наверное, что была Соней, но с тех пор со мною было столько чудес и перемен, что я совсем сбилась с толку.»

«Что ты вздор городишь?» строго остановил её Червяк. «Говори дело!»

«Никак не могу,» отвечает Соня, «потому что я, видите, стала сама не своя.»

«Не вижу,» говорит Червяк.

«Очень жалею,» учтиво продолжает Соня, а саму уже разбирает досада, «Не могу я говорить дело, когда сама не знаю, с чего начать и как объяснить, почему я нынче беспрестанно меняюсь: то стану выше, то ниже. Всё это ужасно бестолково!»

«Нисколько,» говорит Червяк.

«Для вас, может быть, нисколько, а вот посмотрим, каково вам будет, когда вы станете куколкой, а из куколки вылетите бабочкой. Тогда вот увидим, покажется ли вам это странным!»

«Ничуть не странным,» отвечал Червяк.

«Ну, у вас, видно, характер совсем особенный. А мне так оно кажется очень странным.»

«Тебе!» презрительно заметил Червяк, «да кто ты такая?»

«Вот разговор,» думает Соня. «Заладил: кто, да кто?» Досадно ей стало на Червяка, вздумала и его озадачить: выпрямилась во весь свой рост, и с важностью говорит ему: «И вам бы, кажется следовало сказать, *кто вы* такой?»

«Почему это?» кротко спросил Червяк.

Опять Соня стала в тупик: не придумает, почему, и, решив про себя, что Червяк очень не в духе, отвернулась от него и пошла.

«Воротись,» закричал ей Червяк, «я скажу тебе кое-что важное.»

Соня приободрилась, воротилась; подходит.

«Не сердись,» протянул Червяк.

«Только-то!» говорит Соня и так разозлилась, что едва совладала с собою.

«Нет, не только.»

«Впрочем, пусть его,» рассудила Соня; «дела у меня другого нет, послушаю, так и быть,—может, и скажет что-нибудь дельное.» Червяк раза два потянул из трубки, расправил руки, изогнулся и говорит: «Так ты находишь в себе перемену?»

«Нахожу, сударь,» отвечает Соня. «Первое, я ничего порядком не могу припомнить; что ни скажу—всё путаю. Второе, ростом я беспрестанно меняюсь.»

«Что ты именно путаешь?»

«Да вот, хотела сказать наизусть „*Птичку Божию*", так все слова у меня выходят навыворот,» пригорюнившись, отвечает Соня.

«Посмотрим; ну-ка скажи: „*Близко города Славянска…*"»[19]

Соня сложила руки на животик, и начала:—

«Близко города Буянска,
На верху крутой норы,
Пресердитый жил-был парень,
По названию Колотун.

В его погребе глубоком,
Словно мышка в западне,
Изнывала в злом рассоле
Белорыбица душа.

Рано вечером однажды,
У кошачьего окна,
Раскрасавица Катюша,
Притаившися, сидит.

Она плачет, сердце бьётся,
Хочет выскочить оно.
Сердцу чудится отрава
И постыло всё ему.

Вдруг, откуда ни возьмися,
Два мышонка молодых
Наскочили на Катюшку,—
Испугались молодцы!..

Где же парень?—Попивает,
Его слуги также пьют,
Один стриж сидит на крышке
И щебечет про себя.»

«Не так,» сказал Червяк.

«И мне кажется, не совсем так: будто выходят не те слова,» робко сказала Соня.

«Напутала с начала до конца,» решительно сказал Червяк.

Оба замолчали.

«На сколько хочешь вырасти?» заговорил Червяк.

«Мне бы всё равно, лишь бы не меняться беспрестанно; это, знаете, очень скучно.»

«Не знаю,» сказал Червяк.

«Всё дразнится,» думает Соня, и так ей досадно стало, чуть не рассердилась; однако, смолчала.

«Чего тебе ещё надо?»

«Хоть бы мне чуточку прибавить росту, сударь, если можно,» просит Соня, «а то два вершка, что это за рост!»

«Рост прекрасный,» сердито молвил Червяк и вытянулся во всю свою длину (в нём было ровно два вершка).[20]

«Но я ведь к этому не привыкла!» жалобно взмолилась Соня, а сама думает: «Какие же они, право, все обидчивые.»

«Привыкнешь,» протянул Червяк, сунул трубку в рот и принялся курить.

Соня стоит перед ним, терпеливо выжидает, не заговорит ли опять Червяк. Минут чрез пять он выпустил трубку, раза два зевнул, встряхнулся, потом медленно стал спускаться с гриба, и пополз в траву; ползёт и бормочет: «С одного бока отгрызёшь, станешь больше; с другого отгрызёшь—станешь меньше.»

«Чего отгрызть? с чьего бока?» думает озадаченная Соня.

«Гриба,» шепнул Червяк, будто в ответ на её мысль, и вскоре скрылся в густой траве.

«Вот задача, так задача!» раздумалась Соня; глядит на гриб, соображает, с какого бока подойти к нему. Ведь он весь круглый, как тут разберёшь бока! Думала, думала, наконец придумала: обняла гриб обеими руками и каждой рукой отломила от обеих сторон по кусочку.

«Дело теперь в том,» рассуждает она, «от которого кусочка отгрызть, от левого или от правого?» Попробовала от правого—вдруг чувствует удар. Что такое?—Подбородок у неё встретился с ногами. Перепугалась Соня и, не теряя времени, поскорее взялась за кусочек в левой руке; едва справилась разинуть рот, так она вся сплюснулась; однако, приловчилась, кое-как просунула в рот, отгрызла, проглотила…

* * * * *
* * * *
* * * * *

«Ну, слава Богу, голову высвободила!» радостно вскричала Соня. Но недолга была её радость. Глядит, где плечи?—нет их… Ищет Соня плечи, водит повсюду глазами, заглянет вниз—нет; только видно, что длинная-предлинная шея подымается из-под травы высоким стеблем, и ныряет в целом море зелёной листвы.

«И что это за бездна густой зелени? куда я попала?» удивляется Соня. «И куда девались мои плечи? А руки-то, руки—их, бедненьких, совсем не видать!» Соня потрясла руками, чтобы узнать на месте ли они, не увидит ли их? нет, не видать... зашуршали листья где-то внизу, далеко под нею—и только...

Видит Соня, что не поднять ей рук к голове, и догадалась спустить голову к рукам; нагнула шею: шея сгибается и разгибается, точно змеиная. Этому открытию она очень обрадовалась, и плавными, извилистыми движениями стала нырять сквозь веток; тут она поняла, что попала в самые макушки деревьев, подле которых она сперва стояла, когда была маленькая. Вдруг зашипело что-то около неё, и сильно ударило крыльями прямо ей в лицо.

«У-у, змея!» закричал Голубь изо всей мочи.

«Нет, не змея!»

«Змея, змея, змея!» завопила Голубка, но уже тише, и тут же жалобно застонала: «И где я ни пробовала, всё от них не уйдёшь!»

«И о чём ты стонешь, не пойму?» сказала Соня.

«И где я ни пробовала,» не внимая ей, продолжала Голубка стонать, «и в дуплах-то, и на берегу речки, и в плетнях, нет—нигде не упасёшься от этих проклятых змей!»

Слушает Соня, но в толк не возьмёт, на что Голубка жалуется; решилась молчать.

«И так мне хлопот довольно высиживать яйца,» продолжает Голубка, «а тут ещё сторожи денно и нощно, не заползла бы змея! ведь три недели, шутка сказать, я глаз не смыкала!»

«Очень жалко, что вас обеспокоила,» говорит Соня, догадавшись, наконец, в чём дело.

«И только я устроилась на самой макушке самого высокого дерева,» вопит Голубка, «и только я думала, что спаслась от этих злодеек, так нет же, откуда ни возьмись, с неба норовила вильнуть на меня! У-у, змея подколодная!»

«Говорят тебе, я не змея! Какая я змея! я…»

«Кто ж ты такая? говори,» стонет Голубка, «Да ты смотри, не вздумай меня дурачить—нарасскажешь, пожалуй!»

«Я… я… маленькая девочка,» объявила Соня не совсем твёрдым голосом.

«Ну, этому трудно поверить,» с величайшим презрением заметила Голубка. «Много я видала девочек на своём веку, а с такой длинной шеей отроду не доводилось видеть. Нет, ты не девочка, не может этого быть. Какая ты девочка? ты змея! Ты, поди, ещё скажешь, что яиц никогда не едала?»

«Яйца я, конечно, едала,» призналась Соня. (Она была девочка очень правдивая). «Так что ж из этого! Будто девочкам нельзя есть яиц, потому что змеи едят!»

«Что-то не верится. А если так, значит, девочка и змея одного поля ягодки—вот что!»

Соня растерялась, не знает, что отвечать на эти слова. Пока она, молча, собиралась с мыслями, Голубка опять за своё: «Я ведь знаю, зачем ты тут слоняешься,—к моим яйцам пробираешься! И выходит по-моему; что девочка, что змея—одно и то же.»

«А по-моему, вовсе не выходит на одно,» с сердцем выговорила Соня. «Первое, вы ошибаетесь, если воображаете, что я пробираюсь к вашим яйцам; второе, если бы и пробиралась, то, конечно, не стала бы их есть: я не ем, отроду не едала и не стану есть голубиных яиц, особенно сырых!»

«Пусть так, только убирайся!» сердито закричала Голубка, надулась и уселась на гнездо. Соня прижалась к дереву; с непривычки ей было неловко справляться с длинной шеей: она беспрестанно путалась и цеплялась в ветках, и беспрестанно надо было распутывать и отцеплять её. Вдруг она вспомнила, что в руке у неё остался ещё кусочек гриба, нагнула шею к рукам и принялась за грибы: от одного куска погрызёт, от другого откусит: то выше станет, то ниже,—и так она понемногу довела себя до настоящего своего роста.

Сначала даже будто дико показалось ей, что стала настоящей Соней; потом привыкла и заговорила сама с собой, по-старому. «Ну, половина дела у меня теперь сделана. Престранные, однако, были со мной перемены! И теперь не совсем ещё верится, что всё кончено; так и кажется: вот, вот сейчас пойдут какие-нибудь новые штуки. Уж и то хорошо, что я вернула свой прежний рост. Теперь надо непременно добраться до чудесного сада,—как бы это устроить?» Только сказала это Соня, и видит перед собою большую, открытую поляну; на поляне стоит домик всего в аршин вышины. «Кто бы там ни жил,» рассуждает Соня, «не годится мне входить туда: перепугаются моего роста, подумают, великан!» Опять Соня принялась за гриб—убавлять себе росту, и довела себя до полуаршина вышины.[21]

Глава VI

Поросёночек

Соня постояла, поглядела,—не знает, на что решиться. Вдруг, откуда ни возьмись, из лесу выбегает лакей. Соня приняла его за лакея, потому что на нём была ливрея, но голова и лицо у него были рыбьи. Лакей стал громко стучаться кулаком в дверь. Ему отворил другой лакей, круглолицый, глаза навыкате, точь-в-точь лягушка. Очень любопытно стало Соне узнать какое у них дело, и, выбравшись осторожно из лесу, поближе к ним, она стала прислушиваться.

Лакей-Рыба вытащил из-под мышки огромный, чуть ли не с его ростом, конверт и передал его другому лакею. «Пиковой Княгине приглашение от Червонной Крали[22] на игру в крокет,»*[23] важно произнес Лакей-Рыба. Лакей-Лягушка с такой же важностью принял конверт.

Тут оба лакея поклонились друг другу так низко, что стукнулись головами и сцепились курчавыми волосами.

Соня, глядя на них, чуть не расхохоталась вслух, и поскорее убежала в лес, чтобы не заметили её лакеи.

* Игра в шары, в роде лугового бильярда.

Немного погодя, она опять выглянула, видит, Лакей-Рыба ушёл, и сидит один Лакей-Лягушка у двери, на пороге, бессмысленно уставив глаза вверх.

Соня робко подошла, к двери, постучалась.

«Напрасно стучитесь,» сказал Лакей-Лягушка. «Первое, я сижу здесь, и, стало, некому отпереть вам из дому. Второе, у них там идёт такой гам, что никто не услышит, хоть сутки простой.» И вправду, из дому слышался шум необыкновенный: рёв, чихание не умолкали, затем треск, гром, будто кидаются блюдами, или кастрюлями.

«Скажите, пожалуйста, как мне войти в дом?» спросила Соня.

«И что стучаться без толку,» продолжает Лакей своё, будто не слыхал вопроса Сони, «Оно бы ещё можно, кабы вы, примерно, стояли за дверью,—ну, постучались, я бы отпер вам отсюда, а так, знаете...» говорит Лакей и глядит не на Соню, а вверх. «Какой неуч!» думает Соня. «Впрочем, может быть он это не нарочно, а так глаза у него сидят, что не сладит с ними,» одумалась она. «Но хоть бы отвечал на то, что у него спрашивают! Скажите, как мне войти в дом?» уже бойче спрашивает Соня.

«Я здесь, полагать надо, просижу до завтрашнего дня...» опять начинает Лакей.

Вдруг отворяется дверь и вылетает из неё большое блюдо прямо в голову Лакея, задевает его за нос и, ударившись в дерево, разбивается вдребезги.

«...А, может, и больше,» договаривает Лакей тем же голосом, будто ни в чём не бывало.

«Как мне войти?» ещё громче спрашивает Соня.

«Как войти? А за каким вам туда делом, извольте-ка сперва сказать?»

Соне очень не понравилось это замечание. «Ни на что не похоже!» ворчит она, «как эти люди нынче стали рассуждать! не сладишь с ними: совсем из повиновенья вышли!»[24]

А Лакей, с радости должно быть, что огорошил Соню, опять за своё: «А я просижу здесь и ныне и завтра и во веки веков.»[25]

«Но что же мне-то делать?»

«А что угодно,» говорит Лакей, и засвистал.

«Нечего с ним толковать,» говорит Соня, доведённая до отчаяния. «Он набитый дурак!» Пошла, сама отперла дверь и вошла.

Дверь отворялась прямо в большую кухню; в ней стоял дым коромыслом. Посреди кухни, на скамье о трёх ножках, сидела сама Пиковая Княгиня и нянчилась с ребёнком; кухарка, около печки, нагнувшись над огромной кастрюлей, мешала в ней ложкой что-то, похожее на щи.

«Наложила же она в них луку и чесноку,» говорит Соня про себя и расчихалась.

И вправду наложила! По всей кухне стоял запах лука и чеснока; сама Княгиня нет-нет, да и чихнёт; а про ребёнка что и говорить—ревёт да чихает, чихает да ревёт без умолку. Не чихали лишь двое: кухарка да огромная кошка, сидевшая у печки. И что за морда у этой кошки! широкая-прешировкая, будто скалится она до самых ушей.

«Скажите пожалуйста,» начала Соня довольно робко: она не знала, учтиво ли первой вступать в разговор, «отчего это у вас кошка так скалится?»

«Она сибирская кошка,»[26] отвечает Княгиня, «вот отчего. Свинья!..» вдруг крикнула она так яростно, что Соня даже подпрыгнула и оторопела. Увидав, однако, что не её, а ребёнка она обозвала свиньёй, Соня успокоилась и опять пустилась в разговор.

«Я не знала,» говорит она, «что сибирские кошки скалятся. Если правду сказать, я даже совсем не знала, что кошки скалят зубы.»

«Как же, все умеют; все они скалят зубы,» говорит Княгиня.

«Скажите! А я, по правде, никогда этого не видывала и даже совсем не знала,» говорит Соня, и рада, что завела разговор.

«Много ты знаешь! вот это так правда,» сказала Княгиня.

Это замечание не очень-то понравилось Соне, и она стала придумывать другой разговор. Пока она придумывала, кухарка, сняв с огня корчагу со щами, принялась кидать, чем ни попало, в Княгиню и ребёнка: первой полетела кочерга, за нею блюда, тарелки, сковороды, горшки. А Княгиня сидит себе,—ни слова, даже когда попадало в неё чем-нибудь. Ребёнок же и без того так громко ревел, что никак нельзя было разобрать, от боли он ревёт, или так.

«Ах, что это вы! Пожалуйста, перестаньте, осторожнее!» кричит Соня, отскакивая и бегая по кухне в ужасном страхе. «Вот, чуть меня не задели! Ведь эдак можно убить!» уговаривает она кухарку, увертываясь от горшка, который чуть не попал ей в нос. «Велите ей перестать!» обратилась она, наконец, к Княгине.

«Не совался бы каждый в чужие дела, и земля пошла бы шибче кружиться,» заговорила хриплым голосом Княгиня.

«Не знаю, что бы из этого вышло!» говорит Соня, радуясь случаю выказать свою учёность. «Вы только представьте себе, что бы это было, если бы вдруг день перепутался с ночью!.. Ведь земля, знаете, в 24 часа обращается около своей оси…»

«Отстань с твоими часами, счётами да расчётами! Я чисел и цифр терпеть не могу!»

Тут Княгиня занялась ребёнком: качает его и напевает колыбельную песенку.

Споёт стишок, и тряхнёт ребёнка, да так поддаст, что страшно глядеть. На втором стихе Княгиня ещё шибче стала тормошить и подкидывать вверх бедного малютку; а он заливается, визжит, так что за его криком и воем Соня едва могла расслушать:—

«И ревёт-то злой ребёнок,
Только б досадить!
Дам тебе я, поросёнок,
……………………»[27]

«На, можешь понянчиться с ним, коли есть охота,» пропев второй стих, сказала Княгиня и швырнула ребёнком прямо в Соню. «А мне пора собираться к Червонной Крале.» Сказала и проворно пошла к двери. Кухарка пустила в неё сковородою, но промахнулась.

Соня, поймав ребёнка кое-как на лету, сначала едва могла с ним справиться, такой он был неуклюжий, точно чурбан—со всех сторон торчат руки да ноги. Бедняжка пыхтел и фыркал ужасно; ёрзал у неё в руках: то свернётся клубком, то вытянется доской, того и гляди выскользнет. Много было Соне хлопот удержать его на руках!

Наконец, она приловчилась-таки к нему, и, крепко забрав его в охапку, вышла с ним погулять. «Если не отнять у них этого ребёнка, они уморят его непременно; мне надо спасти его от верной смерти!» сказала Соня вслух.

Ребёнок словно хрюкнул. «Что это с ним?» думает удивлённая Соня, и с беспокойством вглядывается ему в лицо. Глядит, а сама думает: «Странный у него, признаться, нос: будто не нос, а скорее рыльце; и глаза что-то уж очень узки!...» Одним словом, не понравилась Соня наружность ребёнка, и даже взяло её сомнение. «Впрочем, это он, может быть, не хрюкал, а рыдал,» утешает она себя, и опять нагнулась, глядит ему в лицо, не видать ли слёз?

Нет, не видать. «Ну,» думает Соня, «если ж ты обернёшься в поросёнка, брошу тебя, непременно брошу! Смотри же!» Малютка опять зарыдал или захрюкал, трудно было разобрать, а Соне всё ещё не совсем верится: ходит она, нянчится с ним, и обдумывает, куда бы ей девать ребёнка, вернувшись в дом.

Как хрюкнет малютка изо всей мочи! даже Соня вздрогнула, взглянула на него,—видит, нет сомнения—не ребёнок, а поросёнок у неё на руках!

Глупо было бы возиться с поросёнком, рассудила Соня и спустила его с рук, а он, к её радости, тотчас отправился мелкой рысцой прямо в лес. Задумалась Соня о том, какие грязные бывают дети, словно поросята; взглянула на дерево, а там сидит Сибирская Кошка: сидит она на сучке, глядит на Соню, ухмыляется.

«Лицом она кажется ничего, добрая,» рассуждает Соня, «но когти у неё уж что-то очень длинные, да острые и зубастая какая,—пожалуй, шутить не любит. Надо с нею осторожно,» решила она.

«Сибирская Киска,» начинает Соня, а сама боится, по нраву ли ей будет это имя. На это Кошка только шире ухмыльнулась. «Кажется, понравилось,» думает Соня. «Не можете ли вы мне сказать,» продолжает она, «куда мне отсюда пройти?»

«А это смотря по тому, куда ты желаешь выйти,» отвечает Кошка.

«Мне бы всё равно, куда…» отвечает Соня.

«А коли всё равно, значит, куда ты ни пойдёшь—везде тебе дорога,» говорит Кошка.

«… лишь бы мне попасть куда-нибудь,» объясняет Соня.

«Ну да; всегда куда-нибудь да попадёшь, покуда носят ноги,» говорит Кошка.

Как с этим не согласиться! Придумала Соня другое. «Скажите,» говорит, «Сибирская Киска, живут ли люди в здешней стороне?»

«Как же, живут. Здесь вот,» говорит, «живёт Враль-Илюшка,[28] а там, Заяц Косой,»[29] и повела в обе стороны лапкой. «Ты у них побывай, оба они шальные.»

«Что мне за охота знакомиться с шальными,» заметила Соня.

«Это не беда,» говорит Кошка, «все мы здесь шальные, и ты, и я, и все мы шальные.»

«Почему вы полагаете, что я шальная?» несколько обидевшись, спрашивает Соня.

«А потому, что ты сюда попала,» решила Кошка.

Соня совсем не была согласна с этим доводом, однако, не желая затевать спора, говорит: «Положим. Но вы-то почему шальная?»

«Сама увидишь. Как, по-твоему: собака шальная или нет?» спрашивает Кошка.

«Не всегда, а только когда взбесится,» отвечает Соня.

«Ну так сама посуди: собака, когда сердится—ворчит, а радуется—виляет хвостом. Я же, напротив, виляю хвостом, когда рассержусь, а радуюсь—ворчу. Как же я не шальная!»

«Кошки, по-моему, курлычат, а не ворчат,» вступилась Соня.

«Это по-твоему; по-моему, курлыкать или ворчать одно и то же,» решила Кошка. «А что, пойдёшь к Червонной Крале на крокет?» вдруг спросила она.

«Не знаю; я не звана, а очень бы хотелось,» говорит Соня.

«Так до свидания, там увидимся,» говорит Кошка: сказала и вдруг исчезла, будто её и не бывало.

Соня за это время мало чему удивлялась,—так она свыклась со всякими странностями. И этому она нисколько не удивилась—а стала озираться, не увидит ли, куда скрылась Кошка. Глядит, она опять на на дереве, на том же сучке.

«Кстати,» говорит Кошка, «чуть не забыла спросить: куда девался ребёнок?»

«Он обернулся в поросёнка,» отвечает Соня.

«Так я и полагала,» говорит Кошка, и опять исчезла.

Соня постояла, подождала, не явится ли она опять, однако, не дождалась, и пошла отыскивать Зайца, куда указала Кошка. «На что мне этот Враль-Илюшка!» рассуждает она, походя. «Зайцы, по-моему, гораздо интереснее.

Посмотрю я на этого; он вовсе, может быть, не такой шальной, как рассказывает Кошка!»

Вскоре завидела она домик; взглянув на него, Соня решила, что это и есть самый дом Зайца: крыша вся крыта заячьими шкурками, вместо трубы торчат ушки. Но дом по её росту оказался слишком велик, потому она тотчас распорядилась прибавить себе росту. Принялась за гриб и грызла его, покуда не поднялась на аршин.[30] Соня тогда подошла к домику, а сама трусит: «Ну, как Заяц в самом деле шальной!» думает она. «И напрасно я, кажется, не пошла к Илюшке!» Подумала, постояла, и решилась войти.

Глава VII

Шальная беседа

Соня вошла в комнату;[31] видит—посредине стоит накрытый, длинный стол; за столом Илюшка с Зайцем сидят за чаем; между ними Мишенька-Сурок[32] спит крепким сном, а те двое, оперши́сь на него локтями, как на подушку, ведут между собой разговор. «Вот нашли себе подушку!» думает Соня, глядя на Мишеньку. «Впрочем, он спит и, должно быть, ничего не чувствует.»

Все трое сидели кучкой на самой середине длинного стола; но лишь только Соня подошла, и собралась сесть за стол, все на неё накинулись, кричат: «Прочь, прочь, места нет!» «Извините, места довольно, даже много лишнего!» отвечает Соня в большом негодовании, и уселась в широкое кресло, на конце стола.

«Не прикажете ли винца?» весьма учтиво предложил ей Заяц.

Соня оглянула весь стол: подан один чай, а вина не видать. «Где же у вас вино?» спрашивает она.

«Вина нет,» говорит Заяц.

«Очень неучтиво с вашей стороны предлагать, чего нет,» с сердцем говорит Соня.

«А с вашей стороны очень неучтиво садиться за стол без приглашения,» отвечает Заяц.

«Вам не мешало бы меня пригласить,—стол накрыт на многих.»

«А вам, Гнеденькая,[33] не мешало бы подстричь гривку!» заметил Илюшка. Он давно уже с любопытством поглядывал на Соню и на длинные её волосы.

«Во-первых, я не Гнеденькая, и таких имён не бывает; во-вторых, вам нет дела до моих волос; а в-третьих, очень неучтиво делать замечания прямо в лицо!» строго обратилась к нему Соня.

[34]

Илюшка на это только вытаращил глаза, и вдруг спрашивает: «А скажите-ка, какая разница между чаем и чайкой?»

«Ну,» думает Соня, «теперь посмеёмся. Хорошо, что он затеял игру в загадки.» «Эту загадку я, кажется, отгадаю,» говорит она вслух.

«То есть, ты думаешь, что придумаешь на неё ответ,» поправил её Заяц.

«Думаю,» отвечает Соня.

«Так говорила бы, что думаешь,» пристаёт Заяц.

«Я и говорю, что думаю,» живо перебивает его Соня. «То есть, я думаю, что скажу—впрочем, это всё равно.»

«Нисколько не всё равно,» вмешался Илюшка. «Эдак, пожалуй, всё равно сказать: „Ем, что вижу, или вижу, что ем!“»

«А я,» говорит Заяц, «скажу: „Ловлю, что люблю, или люблю, что ловлю“,—также всё равно!»

«„Дышу, когда сплю, или сплю, когда дышу“, также выйдет, небось, всё равно?» неожиданно промычал сонный Мишка.

«И прибрал же себе как раз кстати,» заметил Илюшка.[35] Все замолчали. Соня сидела, задумавшись над загадкой, но сколько ни старалась, никак не разгадает.

«Какое нынче число?» вдруг спрашивает Илюшка, и вынул из кармана часы; поглядел на них с беспокойством, стал трясти их, потом приложил к уху.

«Четвёртое,» сказала Соня.

«Так и есть, отстали на два дня!» вздохнул Илюшка. «Говорил я тебе не смазывать их маслом!» сердито обернулся он к зайцу.

«А масло было свежее, *первый* сорт!» кротко заметил Заяц.

«Ну, видно, крошки попали,» ворчит Илюшка. «Говорил я тебе не смазывать хлебным ножом!»

Заяц взял часы, задумчиво стал их осматривать, потом окунул в чашку с чаем и опять внимательно осмотрел. «А масло было *первый* сорт!» повторил Заяц, не придумав иного извинения.

Всё это время Соня следила за происходившим, глядя Зайцу через плечо. «Престранные у вас часы,» говорит она, «показывают не час, а число!»

«Твои разве показывают год?»

«Конечно нет,» отвечает Соня. «Год идёт так долго, что часы не нуж…»

«Ну, вот видишь кто прав?» резко прервал её Илюшка.

Соня совсем растерялась мыслями: она ли не понимает, что говорит Илюшка, а говорит он по-русски; или он говорит бестолково?—ничего не разберёт. «Я что-то вас не понимаю?» как можно учтивее спрашивает Соня.

«Опять Мишенька храпит,» говорит Илюшка, и капнул ему горячим чаем на нос.

Мишенька только тряхнул головой и, не открывая глаз, промычал: «Так, так, разумеется, и я тоже хотел сказать…»

«А загадку разгадала?»

«Нет, никак не могу, скажите разгадку,» отвечает Соня.

«А я почём знаю?»

«И я не знаю,» сказал Заяц.

«Лучше было бы нам и не тратить времени над такими глупостями,» говорит раздосадованная Соня.

«Не тратить времени!» насмешливо повторил Илюшка. «Ты не говорила бы так легкомысленно, если бы была знакома с Временем. Ведь Времени, небось, не знаешь!» Тут Илюшка значительно поднял палец вверх.

«Я ничего не понимаю,» говорит Соня.

«Где ж тебе, Гнеденькая! Ты, видно, не пряха, не ткаха!»[36] с презрением мотнул на неё головой Илюшка. «Ты должно быть, никогда и не имела дела с Временем?»

«Очень может быть,» уклончиво говорит Соня, боясь, что её опять поднимут на смех. «Вот, за уроками разве: мне, признаться, иной раз с временем просто беда—тянется,

тянется и конца ему нет; уж я сижу, сижу... А то в праздник нечего делать бывает,—опять время тянется. Вот тут уж я с ним ужасно бьюсь!»

«Ха-ха-ха! Бьёшься! Ну, оно и понятно, что ты с Временем не в ладу, коли с ним дерёшься. Это дело дрянь! А была бы ты с ним в ладах, какое бы тебе было от него угождение! Сама посуди: примерно, девять часов утра, пора тебе за уроки; а ты только шепнула ему на ухо: не успела оглянуться, уже и стрелки переведены,—глядь, не 9 часов, а половина второго: обедать пора!»

«И как бы пора-то!» заворчал Заяц.

«Это, конечно, было бы славно!» призадумавшись, сказала Соня. «Одно только не совсем ладно: ну, а как я бы ещё не проголодалась к этому времени?»

«Э, пустяки! Время сколько угодно продержит стрелки на половине второго.»

«А вы разве так делаете?» спросила Соня.

«Ни-ни-ни!» замотал Илюшка головой. «С прошлого марта...»

«Не поговорить ли о чём другом,» зевая, вмешался тут Заяц. «Мне-таки этот разговор, признаться, куда как надоел. Не мешало бы этой учёной барышне рассказать нам сказку.»

«Ах, право, я ни одной не знаю!» поторопилась Соня отказаться: очень не понравилось ей такое предложение.

«Так пусть Мишенька расскажет,» закричали оба. «Эй, соня, будет тебе спать!»[37] И пошли его с обоих сторон трепать, щипать, покуда не добудились.

«Я вовсе не спал,» прохрипел Мишенька, едва продирая глаза. «Всё слышал, о чём вы, ребята, толковали…»

«Расскажи сказку,» перебил его Заяц.

«Ах, да, пожалуйста, расскажите сказку,» просит Соня.

«Да проворней начинай, а то, гляди, опять заснёшь,» кричит Илюшка.

«Жили-были три сестрицы,» заторопился Мишенька, «и звали их Сашей, Пашей и Дашей; и жили они в дремучем лесу, под ключом…»[38]

«Как это под ключом? Кто их запер?» в недоумении спрашивает Соня.

«Никто. И сидели они в дремучем лесу под ключом…»

«А что они там кушали?» Соня, надо заметить, вообще очень интересовалась едой и питьём.

«Дрёму,»[39] без запинки отвечает Мишенька.

«Ах, что вы!» живо вступилась Соня. «Дрёма цветок; дрёму не едят! они бы заболели от него.»

«Ну, да, они и заболели, сильно даже хворали, чуть не умерли, а там ничего, поправились,—хворость, знаете, хворостом выбили.»[40]

«Я право, не понимаю, что вы такое говорите? Это выходит сказка совсем ни на что не похожая!»

«Так вы бы не слушали,» напустился на неё Илюшка. «Хотите ещё чаю?»

«Ещё!» обиженно огрызлась Соня. «Довольно странно предлагать *ещё*, когда я ещё не пила!»

«Я и спрашиваю вас, всё ли ещё хотите чаю?»

Соня разобиделась, вышла из-за стола и пошла к двери. Мишенька тотчас заснул, а те двое не обратили на неё никакого внимания. Ещё досаднее стало Соне: она, признаться, ожидала, что попросят её воротиться. Но им было не до того; оглянувшись на них в последний раз, Соня видит: Илюшка с Зайцем, оба изо всех сил хлопочат окунуть Мишеньку мордой в чайник!

«Ноги моей здесь никогда не будет—это верно,» говорит Соня, пробираясь лесом. «Так глупо я в жизни ещё никогда не проводила времени!»

Идёт Соня лесом, видит перед собою дерево; в дереве дверка, и ведёт дверка прямо в дерево. Штука странная, но Соне не привыкать стать к странностям! Не задумавшись, она отпирает дверку, входит в дерево.

Что это? Куда она попала? Глядит, опять прежняя, длинная зала; на прежнем месте стоит хрустальный столик;

на столике золотой ключик. «Погоди,» думает Соня, «теперь я распоряжусь умнее.» Сперва взяла со стола ключик, потом отперла им дверку, выходящую в сад, и тогда только, вынув из кармана кусочек гриба, лежавший у неё в запасе, стала грызть его помаленьку, осторожно, покуда не довела себя до уровня дверки. Какова была радость Сони, когда, пробравшись коридорчиком, она вышла, наконец, в чудесный сад, где пышно цвела и благоухала бездна ярких цветов, где искрились и били светлые, прохладные фонтаны!

Глава VIII

Игра в крокет

В саду, у самого входа, высоко подымался огромный куст, весь усыпанный белыми розами в полном цвету. Около него трое садовников с кистями в руках усердно хлопотали, закрашивая белые розы в красный цвет. Эта затея удивила Соню. «Престранную они придумали штуку,» думает Соня, и подошла поближе на них посмотреть. Слышит, один говорит: «Эй, Пятёрка, берегись, всего меня обрызгал краской!»

«Не я виноват—вон Семёрка толкнула меня под локоть.»

«Так, так, Пятёрка, всегда сваливай с больной головы да на здоровую,» говорит Семёрка и сердито взглянула на Пятёрку.

«Уж ты бы молчал,» говорит Пятёрка: «слышал, намедни приказывала её милость снести тебе голову?»

«За что это?» спросил первый садовник.

«Не твоё дело,» говорит Семёрка.

«Нет, его дело,» говорит Пятёрка. «Я вот скажу за что. За то, что на царскую кухню отпустил цветочных луковиц вместо луку—вот за что!»

Семёрка с досады бросила кисть, да как закричит: «Вот уж напраслина, так…»—да вдруг, увидав Соню, замолчала и уставилась на неё, разиня рот. И те двое её тогда заметили, и все трое низко ей поклонились.

«Скажите, пожалуйста,» робко начала Соня, «для чего вы закрашиваете белые розы в красный цвет?»

Пятёрка с Семёркой молча оглянулись на Двойку, а эта говорит, да так почтительно, вполголоса: «Изволите видеть, барышня, приказано было на этом месте посадить куст с красными розами, а по нечаянности посадили белых. Как увидит их милость, Червонная Краля, всем нам велит головы снести. Вот мы и стараемся поправить беду до них.» Пока говорила Двойка, Пятёрка, в большой тревоге, глядела всё в одном направлении, и вдруг закричала: «Идут, идут! Червонная Краля идёт!» Тут все трое садовников ударились лицом в землю. Послышался топот, как от множества людских ног. Соня встрепенулась в радостном ожидании.

Вот идут: сперва выступили парами десять пиковых солдат, и все они, как вылитые, похожи на трёх садовников: такие же плоские, продолговатые, все стоят вверх и вниз головами, руки справа и слева по углам. За ними также парами шли десять придворных валетов, разукрашенные бубнами. За валетами шли царские дети; их также было десятеро, и все они, милашки, разодетые с червонными сердцами, шли парами, держа друг друга, за ручки, и весело подпрыгивали. За ними следовали приглашённые гости, короли и придворные дамы. Между гостями, кого же узнаёт Соня?—старого знакомого, Беленького Кролика! Он шёл торопливо, будто сам не свой; то заговорит, то поклонится и такой перепуганный, растерянный, что, проходя мимо Сони, не заметил её. За гостями шёл Червонный Валет и на бархатной подушке нёс царскую корону. В самом конце шествия выступали КОРОЛЬ И КРАЛЯ ЧЕРВОННЫЕ.

Соня было подумала, не следует ли и ей пасть перед ними ниц, но, вспомнив, что нигде не читала о таком обыкновении при церемониальных выходах, решила глядеть на него стоя. «Да и некому было бы любоваться на эти интересные церемонии, если бы все лежали, уткнувшись лицом в землю,» рассудила она.

Когда шествие поравнялось с Соней, все остановились и стали глядеть на неё, а Червонная Краля обратилась к Червонному Валету и спрашивает: «Это кто такая?» На это Червонный Валет только осклабился и зашаркал ногами.

«Болван!» закричала на него раздосадованная Червонная Краля, замотала головой и сама к Соне: «Как тебя,» говорит, «милая, звать?»

«Меня, Ваше Величество, зовут Соней,» почтительно отвечает Соня, а сама думает: «Ах, батюшки! Да это всё карты, карточные короли да крали! чего мне их бояться!»

«А эти, вон, кто такие?» спрашивает Червонная Краля, указывая на садовников: они лежали лицом к земле, а по рубашкам нельзя было узнать, солдаты, валеты, или царские они дети.

«Я не знаю, да и не моё это дело знать!» отвечает Соня, и сама подивилась своей смелости.

Червонная Краля побагровела от гнева, услышав такой ответ.

Соня не струсила и смело глядела ей в глаза.

Червонная Краля хотела что-то крикнуть, но замолчала.

«Сама рассуди, душенька, она ведь ребёнок,» робко вступился Король за Соню, кротко положив руку Червонной Крале на плечо.

Она с гневом отвернулась от Короля и, указывая на лежавших садовников, говорит Валету: «Обернуть их лицом!»

Валет приподнял их ногой и обернул лицом.

«На ноги, фофаны!»[41] резко прикрикнула краля на них, и садовники горошком вскочили на ноги и принялись кланяться на все стороны: Королю, Крале, царским детям и всем придворным.

«Будет, будет, болваны! Совсем завертелись!» Червонная Краля отвернулась, увидала красные розаны, взглянула на них и говорит: «Это что наделано?»

Двойка опустилась на коленки и говорит дрожащим голосом: «Это, изволите видеть… вашей милости угодно было приказать… мы изволили стараться…»

«Вижу, вижу, вы изволили постараться,» передразнила её Червонная Краля, осматривая куст и погрозила кулаком. Шествие двинулось вперёд. Отстало от него лишь трое солдат, чтобы исполнить приговор над бедными садовниками, которые бросились к Соне, умоляя защитить их.

«Не бойтесь, останетесь целы,» сказала им Соня; взяла и сунула всех троих в цветочный горшок. Солдаты поискали, поискали и, недоискавшись их, преспокойно отправились себе назад.

«Умеешь ты играть в крокет?» вдруг крикнула Краля.

Солдаты молча взглянули на Соню, догадавшись, что к ней обратилась Червонная Краля с вопросом.

«Умею,» отвечала Соня.

«Так иди сюда,» заревела Краля, и Соня пошла за шествием.

«Прекрасная нынче погода,» запищал кто-то тоненьким голоском около Сони; она оглянулась,—видит, Беленький Кролик идёт и заглядывает ей в лицо.

«Да, погода прекрасная,» говорит Соня. «А где Пиковая Княгиня?»

«Ш-ш, молчи, ради Бога!» шепчет Кролик, а сам боязливо озирается на все стороны. Потом, поднявшись на цыпочки, он шепчет ей на ухо: «Не знаешь разве, она была под судом, приговорена к смерти!»

«За что это?» спрашивает Соня.

«Ты говоришь, „Как жаль это?“» переспросил Кролик.

«Совсем я этого не говорила! Чего мне её жалеть! Я сказала: „За что это?“»

«Тишс, тише, ради Бога! Ну как услышит *она*! Это, видишь, как случилось: позвала она Пиковую Княгиню к себе на вечер играть, а та чуть-чуть опоздала; и говорит ей *она*…»

«По местам!» заревела тут Червонная Краля на всю площадь. Все испугались, переполошились,—словно громом оглушило всех. Поднялась беготня, толкотня: одни наскакивали на других, сшибали друг друга с ног, кидались опрометью вперёд, летели кувырком чрез головы, и чего-чего тут не было! Однако, стали униматься понемногу; пришли в себя, устроился порядок, началась игра.

Но что за игра! Такой игры Соня никогда не видывала! Площадка вся неровная: где доска гнилая, где торчит ребром, а где вовсе провалилась.[42] Вместо шаров живые ежи; вместо арок—картонные солдаты стоят друг у друга на голове, перегнувшись в три погибели, вместо молотков— живые журавли.

Главным затруднением для Сони было справляться с своим журавлём: никак не приноровится схватить его половчее: только она его возьмёт на руки, он норовит вывернуться, просунет длинную шею ей под руку и глядит в глаза, да так смешно, что Соня расхохочется. Пока она опять укладывает его и, дождавшись очереди, идёт играть, смотрит: либо ежи сбежали в сторону, либо пустились в драку.

Поглядела, поглядела Соня, да и решила, что труднее этой игры ничего не придумаешь. Игроки беспрестанно путались; играли все разом, не дожидаясь очереди, и спорили из-за ежей.

Соня стала озираться, нет ли где лазейки, куда бы незаметно скрыться. Подняла глаза,—что за диво! В воздухе стала показываться морда с оскаленными зубами! «Это, должно быть, Сибирская Кошка,» догадалась Соня и очень обрадовалась, что будет с кем поболтать.

«Как поживаешь?» говорит Кошка, лишь только вышло довольно морды, чтобы можно было говорить.

Соня дождалась, покуда у Кошки вышли глаза и думает: «Пусть ещё выйдут уши, а то что пользы говорить: пожалуй, не услышит!» Наконец явилась вся голова и на этом стала. Соня рада, что есть кому её слушать, и пустилась рассказывать об игре в крокет.

«И как они бестолково играют,» жалобно начала Соня, «вы себе представить не можете! Никакого порядка; никто никого не слушает; говоришь,—самого себя не расслышать; ссорятся, дерутся, спорят, никаких правил не соблюдают. С молотками и шарами—беда! Все живые, перебегают с места на место; хватишься шара, а он куда-то уполз, поди, ищи его. Не поверите, как трудно! С одними журавлями голова кругом идёт. Вот я бы непременно выиграла партию у Червонной Крали; гляжу, где мой шар—а он вцепился в драку с чужим ежом—ну, разнимать надо!»

«А как тебе нравится Червонная Краля?» вполголоса спрашивает Кошка.

«Совсем не нравится,» говорит Соня. «У неё, знаете, такой ужасный...» Тут Соня замечает, за плечом у неё стоит Червонная Краля, прислушивается. Струсила Соня,—однако, тотчас нашлась, поправила себя, говорит: «...такое ужасное счастье, что играть с нею невозможно!»

На это Краля самодовольно улыбнулась и пошла дальше.

«С кем это ты разговариваешь?» спрашивает Король, подойдя к Соне.

«Это знакомая мне Сибирская Киска,» говорит Соня. «Позвольте мне её вам представить.»

«Морда её мне вовсе не нравится,» говорит Король, «однако, если желает, пусть приложится к моей руке.»

«Избавьте от чести,» сухо сказала Кошка.

«Не груби, смотри! Чего ты пялишь на меня глазища!» сказал Король и стал Соне за спину.

«И чего она здесь торчит! вовсе не у места,» решил он. «Прикажи её, душенька, отсюда убрать,» обратился он к Червонной Крале.

Соня видит, здесь ей делать нечего, пошла взглянуть на игроков: трое из них уже были приговорены к смерти. Слышит издали: крик, гам—это бушует Червонная Краля. Соня подходит, видит: игроки все перебунтовались. Что ей делать!

Пошла отыскивать своего ежа да журавля; застаёт их в драке с другим ежом да журавлями. «Самое время,» думает Соня, «схватить их!» Поймала обоих, ежа завернула в платок, журавля сунула под мышку, стала дожидаться своей очереди.

Дождалась, опять беда! Валеты соскочили друг у друга с головы, борются, повалились, а остальные сбежались их разнимать. У Сони с досады опустились руки. Пока приводили всё в порядок, Соня опять хватилась ежа—нет его; выскользнул из платка! куда девался? Соня глядит, ищет, а он вон где:—в сад уполз, забрался в самую глушь, шуршит там, роется в куче сухих листьев. Она за ним; поймала, уложила, притащила к крокету, а на крокете уже никого нет: игра кончилась.

«Пожалуй,» рассуждает Соня, «не стоило и доигрывать такой бестолковой партии!» Она завязала ежа в платок и хотела уходить, но вдруг перед ней Пиковая Княгиня, да такая добрая.

Глава IX

Соня в зверинце

«Уж как же я рада тебя видеть, душенька!» говорит Пиковая Княгиня и, взяв Соню под руку, пошла с нею прохаживаться.

И Соня рада, что Пиковая Княгиня теперь в хорошем расположении духа.

«От лука и чеснока, должно быть, она была такая сердитая давеча, в кухне! Когда я буду княгиней, никогда не позволю держать чеснок на кухне,» решила Соня. «И на что он! в суп никуда не годится, только портит. Вот сахар и леденец другое дело! От него дети бывают такие добренькие, кроткие; если б знали это большие, не стали бы так скупиться на него.»

И Соня очень была довольна, что додумалась до такой премудрости; и так она раздумалась о леденце и сахаре, что совсем забыла о подруге своей, Пиковой Княгине, даже вздрогнула, когда та закричала ей на ухо: «О чём ты, душенька, так задумалась, что забыла про меня? Из этого выходить нравоучение, что бишь… погоди, дай вспомнить!»

«Может быть, и ничего из этого не выходит?» заметила Соня.

«Что ты, что ты, дитятко! Изо всего всегда можно вывесть нравоучение,—надо только придумать его.» И Пиковая Княгиня ещё крепче обняла Соню.

А Соне вовсе это не нравилось по двум причинам: первое—Пиковая Княгиня была ужасно дурна собой; второе—она упиралась ей подбородком прямо в плечо, а подбородок у ней был преострый. Однако, не желая быть неучтивой, Соня решилась терпеть.

«Игра, кажется пошла на лад,» говорит Соня, чтобы завязать разговор.

«Как же, как же,» поддакнула Пиковая Княгиня. «Отсюда нравоученье: „Любовью свет держится!“»

«А я так слыхала, что дело мастера боится,» пролепетала Соня.

«Пожалуй, и так: это почти одно и то же,» согласилась Пиковая Княгиня. «Отсюда нравоученье: „Лишь бы был смысл, а слова сами придут“.» Тут она опять ткнулась острым подбородком в плечо Соне.

«И что она за охотница ко всякому слову причитывать!» думает Соня.

«Я рада бы ещё крепче тебя обнять, чтобы доказать тебе свою дружбу,» вдруг говорит Пиковая Княгиня, «да вот зверёк, что у тебя в платке, что-то очень топорщится, как бы его не раздразнить!»[43]

«Пожалуй, раздразнишь, может уколоть,» поспешила сказать Соня, вовсе не желая обниматься с Княгиней.

«Правда, правда, и я слыхала, что ёж, что горчица, больно кусаются… Отсюда нравоученье, что свой своему поневоле брат!»

«Но ведь горчица не животное,» заметила Соня.

«Опять-таки твоя правда,» говорит Княгиня. «И что ты за умница? Слово скажешь—рублём подаришь!»

«Горчица, кажется, из царства ископаемых,» говорит Соня.

«Разумеется,» говорит Княгиня, которая, казалось, готова была согласиться со всем, что ни скажет Соня. «Вот даже неподалёку отсюда есть горчичные копи, как же не ископаемое! Отсюда выходит, что сколько ни копи, довольно не накопишь!»

«Ах, знаю теперь, вспомнила!» закричала Соня, не расслыхав последних слов Княгини. «Горчица из царства растительного: это овощ, хоть видом и не похожа на растение.»

«И на этот раз совершенно согласна с тобою,» говорит Княгиня. «Отсюда нравоученье: „Будь тем, чем хочешь“; проще говоря: „Всегда будь такою, какою желаешь казаться другим, но так, чтобы не заметили другие, что ты желаешь казаться такою, какою ты желаешь показаться другим, а чтобы думали другие, что ты действительно такая, какою желаешь казаться!“»

«Если бы вы потрудились мне это записать, оно было бы мне понятнее, а то я никак не могу поспеть за вами, все слова перепутались,» говорит Соня как можно учтивее.

«О, это что! пустяки в сравнении с тем, что я могу сказать, если захочу!» говорит Княгиня и самодовольно улыбнулась.

«Нет, уж пожалуйста не трудитесь: хорошенького понемножку,—и то уж у меня голова совсем закружилась,» поспешила Соня отказаться.

«Какой это труд, душенька! Я даже от всей души готова подарить тебе каждое своё слово!»

«Дешёвый подарок!» думает Соня. «Беда, если бы так дарили к рождению и именинам!»

«Опять задумалась!» говорит Княгиня и ткнула ей подбородком в плечо.

«Никто, кажется, не запрещает мне думать,» резко говорит Соня: ей сильно стало надоедать приставание Пиковой Княгини.

«Что ты, что ты, миленькая! ни тебе мечтать, ни свинье летать—никто не вправе запретить! И выходит из э….»

На этом, к удивленно Сони, голос Пиковой Княгини разом оборвался, и она вся затряслась; Соня взглянула—перед ними, скрестивши руки, стоит Червонная Краля, насупившись, словно грозная туча.

«Погода нынче прекрасная, Ваше Величество!» запищала Пиковая Княгиня чуть слышным трепетным голоском.

«Погоди!.. я тебе покажу погоду!» заорала Червонная Краля, и топнула ногой.

Пиковая Княгиня, долго не думая, давай Бог ноги!

«Пойдёшь теперь доигрывать партию,» обратилась к Соне Червонная Краля. А Соня, глядя на них, так перетрусила, что стоит сама не своя, и молчком побрела за Кралей.

Тем временем игроки, пользуясь отсутствием Крали, расположились под деревьями отдыхать. Лишь завидели они её, повскакали с мест, и назад к крокету! а Червонная Краля ну их подгонять!

Вдруг Червонная Краля, раскрасневшись, запыхавшись, говорит Соне: «А видела ты мой зверинец?»

«Нет,» отвечала Соня, «что это за зверинец?»

«А вот увидишь; все они идут ко мне на кухню.»[44]

«Такого зверинца я никогда не видывала,» говорит Соня.

«Ну, так увидишь; пойдём, они сами тебе расскажут про себя.»

Первый попавшийся им зверь был Грифон. Пригревшись на солнце, он спал, свернувшись клубком. (Если не знаете, что за зверь Грифон, взгляните на картинку.) «На ноги, лентяй!» закричала на него Червонная Краля. «Сведи эту барышню к Телячьей Головке.» И она бросила Соню одну, глаз на глаз с Грифоном. Соня крепко не понравилась наружность этого зверя; однако, подумавши, она решила, что вернее, пожалуй, остаться с ним, чем идти за этой свирепой Червонной Кралей. Стала Соня и ждёт.

Грифон протер себе глаза, поглядел Крале вслед и, когда она скрылась из виду, загоготал: «Шутиха!» не то про себя, не то вслух.

«Кто это шутиха?» спросила Соня.

«Конечно, она!» сказал Грифон. «Всё у неё одно воображение!.. всё грозит снести голову! никому никогда не сносили головы—все целёхоньки! ну, как же не шутиха! иди сюда!»

«Отроду так мною не командовали!» думает Соня и потихоньку пошла за Грифоном.

Немного они прошли, как завидели «Телячью Головку».[45] Из брони черепахи торчала телячья голова; хвост и задние ноги—телёнка, передние лапы—черепахи. Грустно и одиноко сидела она на обломке скалы. Подойдя к ней поближе, Соня слышит: вздыхает Телячья Головка, будто сердце у неё надрывается. Разжалобилась Соня над ней. «О чём она грустит?» спрашивает она Грифона, а Грифон говорит: «Всё это у неё одно воображение, никакого горя у неё нет. Подойдём к ней.»

Подошли, а Телячья Головка только глядит на них большими заплаканными глазами, ничего не говорит.

«Вот барышня пришла послушать твои россказни,» говорит ей Грифон.

«Пожалуй, расскажу,» глухим голосом, мрачно выговорила Телячья Головка. «Садитесь оба и не говорите ни слова, покуда я не кончу.»

Уселись и молчат. Долго ли, нет ли они молчали, только Соне начало надоедать так сидеть.

«Однажды,» замычала, наконец, Телячья Головка, и тяжело вздохнула, «я была настоящим телёнком.»

За этим настало долгое молчание: Телячья Головка опять зарыдала, а Грифон передразнивает её,—так же всхлипывает. Соня потеряла терпение и собралась было уходить, поблагодарить за приятную беседу, но ей вдруг стало жалко Телячью Головку и она решилась подождать; уселась опять и молчит.

«И жилось нам хорошо, телятам, как вздумали вдруг сделать из нас черепах и отдали нас в ученье к старой черепахе, жившей в море,» несколько успокоившись и лишь изредка всхлипывая, продолжает Телячья Головка. «Море это было не настоящее, а солёный бассейн, но мы его называли морем.»

«Почему же вы его называли морем, когда оно было не настоящее?» спросила Соня.

«Мы его называли морем, потому что нас там морили,»[46] сердито отвечала Телячья Головка. «И воспитывали нас прекрасно…»

«Я тоже хожу в школу, нечего вам, стало быть, так хвастаться!» прерывает Соня.

«А есть у вас дополнительные предметы за особую плату?» хвастливо спросила Телячья Головка.

«Как же, французский и музыка.»

«А стирке вас учат?»

«Какой вздор! конечно, не учат,» с негодованием говорит Соня.

«Ну, хороша же эта *ваша* школа! самая пустая!» решительно выговорила Телячья Головка и самодовольно вздохнула. «Нет, у нас учили.»

«Что же вы стирали? ведь вы жили в воде?» насмешливо заметила Соня.

«По бедности я не могла этому обучаться,» вздохнула Телячья Головка. «Ну, чему же вас учат?»

«Нас сначала учат читать, потом идут склонение, спряжение…»[47]

«Да, да, да,» подхватила Телячья Головка, «слоняние, наряжание…»

«А по скольку часов в день вас учили?» поторопилась Соня повернуть разговор, видя, что Головка понесла чепуху.

«По десяти часов в первый день, по девяти—на второй, и так далее, всё на ущерб.»

«Скажите, какой странный порядок?» удивилась Соня.

«Ничего не странно! Сама увидишь. Ведь иначе никогда не отучишься. Вот понемногу ученье-то и убавлялось.»

Такая новая мысль очень заняла Соню; она задумалась над ней и собралась было с новым вопросом.

Глава X

Раковая пляска

Телячья Головка глубоко вздохнула, провела лапой по глазам, поглядела на Соню, будто желая что-то сказать, но рыдания заглушили ей голос. «Ни дать, ни взять подавилась костью!» говорит Грифон, и ну её тормошить и колотить в спину. После этой трёпки Телячья Головка пришла в себя; слёзы всё ещё текли по её щекам, однако она успокоилась настолько, что могла проговорить:

«Ты, может быть, не живала на дне морском, и потому не имела случая познакомиться с морским раком?»

«Случалось его пробовать, когда подавали к сто…» начала было Соня, но поскорее замолчала, боясь кого-нибудь обидеть. «Никогда не случалось,» говорит она.

«Следственно, ты никак не можешь себе представить всю прелесть раковой пляски!»

«Никак не могу,» согласилась Соня. «Что это за пляска?»

«Не желаешь ли посмотреть,—мы, пожалуй, пропляшем?» предложил Грифон.

«С удовольствием.»

«Давай, пропляшем первую фигуру!» говорит Грифон Телячьей Головке.

Телячья Головка утёрла слёзы и охотно согласилась.

Начали: пошли кружиться около Сони, то заденут её хвостом, то отдавят ей ногу.

«Благодарю вас, очень занимательная эта пляска!» говорит Соня, а сама ждёт не дождётся конца.

Наконец кончили.

«Ты бы рассказала нам теперь про свои приключения,» обратился вдруг Грифон к Соне.

«С удовольствием расскажу вам, что было со мною, но только с сегодняшнего дня,» робко начала Соня. «Про вчерашний не стоит говорить, потому что вчера я была совсем не той, чем стала нынче с утра.»

«Что-то непонятно—объясни,» говорит Телячья Головка.

«Прошу без объяснений; от них одна скука. Начинай прямо с приключений,» говорит Грифон.

И пошла Соня им рассказывать, что было с нею с тех пор, как, увидавши Белого Кролика, она погналась за ним. Сначала она робела и несколько сбивалась и было с чего: оба зверя подсели близко к ней и, широко разинув пасть, выпучили на неё глаза. Вскоре, однако, она оправилась и стала говорить смелей. Слушатели её сидели смирно, чинно и не прерывали её, покуда не дошла она до того места, где Червяк велел ей прочитать наизусть «*Близко города Славянска*» и слова у неё выходили все навыворот.

«Оказия!» проговорила тут Телячья Головка и глубоко вздохнула.

«Да, признаться,—оказия!» поддакнул Грифон.

«И всё выходило навыворот?» задумчиво переспросила Телячья Головка. «Любопытно было бы её прослушать; вели-ка ей сказать что-нибудь,» обратилась она к Грифону, словно он более её имел права командовать Соней.

«Встань и прочитай наизусть „*Раз в крещенский вечерок…*“» приказал Грифон.

«И они туда же распоряжаться! задавать уроки! это выходит, ни дать ни взять, та же школа!» думает Соня, однако встала, начала. И понесла она такую чепуху, что и сама себя не разберёт: пляшут у неё в голове поросята, разные звери, а язык болтает,—не сладит она с ним никак:

«Раз, собравшися в кружок,
Петухи гадали,
На ворота колпачок,
Сняв с ноги, сажали…»[48]

Соня остановилась—стыдно ей и досадно стало; она закрыла лицо руками и думает: «Будет ли всей этой чепухе конец?»

«Не мешало бы тебе объяснить,» начала было Телячья Головка, но Грифон перебил её.

«Где ей,» говорит, «объяснять! И сама-то себя не разберёт.»

«Не желаешь ли, мы пропляшем тебе вторую фигуру раковой кадрили? А то, не попросишь ли Телячью Головку спеть нам песенку?» предложил Грифон.

«Ах, да, пожалуйста, песенку! Будьте так добры, спойте что-нибудь,» говорит Соня Телячьей Головке.

Телячья Головка тяжело вздохнула и дрожащим голосом, прерываемым рыданьем, затянула:—

«Ах, прекраснейший суп
Из головки телячьей!..»[49]

Только что заголосила Телячья Головка, как вдруг издали послышался крик: «К суду, к суду; допрос начался!»

«Идём!» заторопился Грифон, и, не дождавшись конца песни, схватил Соню за руку и пустился бежать.

«Какой допрос? кого судят?» допрашивает Соня, едва переводя дух; а Грифон только пуще торопит её и сам шибче бежит. Издалека, всё слабее и слабее доносились до них замирающие звуки жалобной песни Телячьей Головки:

«Ах, прекраснейший суп
Из головки телячьей!..»

Глава XI

Заседание суда

На троне сидели Король и Краля Червонные; около них собралась большая толпа из мелких пташек и всяких зверят; тут же выстроилась вся колода карт. Подсудимый, Червонный Валет, в цепях стоял перед троном, охраняемый двумя стражами. Возле Короля Белый Кролик держит в одной руке звонок, в другой—большой свёрток бумаги. На средине залы, на стол было поставлено большое блюдо с сладкими пирожками. И что за вкусные пирожки! Глядя на них, у Сони глаза и зубы разгорелись.

Соня никогда ещё не бывала в заседаниях суда, но слыхала толки о них. «Этот вот—судья, потому, что у него цепь на груди,»[50] думает Соня. А на этот раз судьёй был сам Король.

«А там вон скамья, а на ней сидят всё разные животные. Это, должно быть, пристяжные,» подумала Соня. Она, видите, говорила «пристяжные», потому что не совсем затвердила слово *присяжные*.[51] «Да, это пристяжные, пристяжные,» повторяла она с самодовольствием несколько раз кряду, а сама думает: «Это, пожалуй, знает не каждая девочка одних со мною лет!»

Эти двенадцать *пристяжных* усердно строчили что-то на грифельных досках. «Что они пишут? И о чём им писать, когда суд ещё не начался?» шепнула Соня на ухо Грифону.

«Имена свои учатся подписывать, не равно забудут до окончания суда,» шепнул ей Грифон в ответ.

«Глупыя тва…!» крикнула Соня, но испугалась и остановилась на полслове. «Тише, господа!» громко крикнул Белый Кролик. Король надел очки и с досадой оглянул собрание.

Соня с своего места заметила как все присяжные записали на своих досках: «глупыя тва..!» Ещё ей показалось, что один из присяжных не знал: писать ли «глуп*ые*» или «глуп*ыя*», и шептался об этом с соседом. «Ну, славная у них выйдет каша на досках!» думает Соня.

У одного из присяжных грифель нестерпимо визжал; этого не выдержала Соня,—встала, прокралась задними рядами к скамье присяжных, стала за виновным, и, дождавшись удобного случая, выхватила у него грифель. Она сделала это так ловко и проворно, что бедненький, маленький присяжный не догадался, куда девался его грифель. Поискал, поискал, искоса посмотрел на Кралю, и пошёл водить пальцем по доске. Хоть мало из этого толку, а всё же на вид как будто дело делает.

Вдруг дверь с шумом отворилась, и в залу ввалился Враль-Илюшка; в одной руке у него чашка чая, в другой—кусок хлеба. «Прощения просим, Ваше Величество,» обратился он к Королю, «я сидел за чаем, да вижу, что пора идти, ну и захватил чашечку. И тут можно допить.»

«Шляпу долой!» закричал на него Король.

«Никак невозможно, Ваше Величество,» говорит Илюшка, «я шляпами торгую, изволите видеть,—шляпа у меня служит вывеской.»

Тут Червонная Краля надела очки и выпялила глаза на Илюшку, да так страшно, что Илюшка побледнел и весь затрясся.

«Шляпу долой, болван!» повторил Король, «не то, берегись, велю тебя казнить!»

Илюшка беспокойно поглядывал на Червонную Кралю и переминался с ноги на ногу. Кончилось тем, что вместо хлеба он с испугу выкусил большой кусок из чашки.

А Червонная Краля не спускала глаз с Илюшки и вдруг как закричит: «Что ему надо? зачем пришёл?» Илюшка ещё пуще перепугался,—едва на ногах держится, даже башмаки растерял.

«Чего тебе надо, зачем пришёл?» повторил Король. «Сейчас отвечай, не то казнить велю тебя, трусишка негодный!»

«Я, Ваше Величество, бедный человек,» дрожащим голосом начал Илюшка. «И только я садился за чай, и всего-то я с неделю сидел, а может и меньше—за хлопотами запамятовал!»

«Что ты городишь!» крикнул на него Король.

Бедный Илюшка с испуга выронил из рук чашку, хлеб и пал на колени:

«Я, Ваше Величество, бедный человек…» начал было он.

«И негодный болтун, пустомеля!» огорошил его Король.

Тут захихикали и одобрительно захрюкали заморские свинки; но их тотчас

укротили: сунули в мешок, связали его и положили под скамью.

«От тебя, я вижу, толку не добьёшься, убирайся! Ну, живо, проваливай!» сказал Король.

А Илюшка, всё лежит, припав лицом к полу.

«Куда же мне ещё провалиться!» жалобно вопит бедняга, «уж и так лежу!.. Ваше Величество!» вдруг, с отчаяния, вскрикнул он, несколько приподняв голову, «окажите божескую милость, отпустите к чаю!» А сам боязливо, исподлобья глядит на Червонную Кралю.

«Отпустить его!» решил Король. Илюшка мигом вскочил и без башмаков—давай бог ноги.

Вдруг Соня слышит—резкий голос зовет: «Соня!»

Глава XII

Показания Сони

«Я здесь,» громко отвечает удивлённая Соня, вскакивает на ноги и стремительно бросается вперёд. Забыв про свой огромный рост, она впопыхах задела ногой скамью присяжных. Скамья повалилась, и присяжные кувырком полетели во все стороны, карабкаясь и барахтаясь в ужасном смятении.

«Ах, простите, извините... Это я нечаянно!» жалобно завопила Соня и бросилась подбирать присяжных и усаживать их, как попало, по скамьям.

«Нельзя начинать допрос, покуда не будет всё в порядке!» строго выговорил Король и значительно взглянул на Соню.

Соня оглянулась на скамью присяжных и видит, что второпях она сунула бедного Ваську-таракана вверх ногами. Черномазенький лежит на спине и беспомощно болтает ножками в воздухе. Соня нагнулась, обернула его, осторожно взяла двумя пальцами за спинку, посадила на скамью, а сама думает:

«А вы, друзья, как ни садитесь,
Всё в музыканты не годитесь!»[52]

И так ей стало смешно, что она едва удержалась, чтобы не расхохотаться вслух.

Лишь только присяжные несколько пришли в себя, они отыскали доски и грифеля и снова принялись усердно писать свои имена. Один Васька не писал, а сидел, как одурелый. Соня стояла так близко к ним, что могла заглядывать им в доски и видела, что они все исписаны одними именами.

Соня не выдержала и захихикала.

В эту минуту Король, который усердно записывал что-то в памятную книжку, вдруг поднял голову, окинул взором собрание и крикнул: «Молчание!» Все притихли. Он опять заглянул к себе в книжку и говорит: «По статье 42-й лица, превышающие установленную законом меру, не могут присутствовать в заседании присяжных. Соня, удались! в тебе сажень росту.[53] Ты превышаешь меру.»

Все взглянули на Соню. И в самом деле она похожа была на колокольню посреди этого собрания, и надо было высоко поднимать голову, чтобы взглянуть ей в лицо.

«Во мне нет сажени,» защищается Соня.

«Есть,» говорит Король.

«Больше сажени!» кричит Червонная Краля, «вон, вон, вон сейчас!»

«Сажень ли, две ли сажени, это как вам угодно, а я из собрания не выйду!» горячится Соня. «И статьи такой вовсе нет, а сами вы её сейчас сочинили!»

«Статья эта существует спокон века, из первых первейшая,» гневно возражает Король.

«Ну, и выходит, что ваша статья не 42-я, а 1-я,» отвечает Соня, всё более горячась.

Король побледнел и с досадой захлопнул памятную книжку.

«Молчать!»

«Вздор! Не замолчу!» закричала Соня вне себя.

«Снести ей голову!» во всё горло заорала Червонная Краля.

Никто не двинулся.

«Очень я вас боюсь!» гордо и смело сказала Соня. «Все-то вы колода карт и больше ничего—годны разве только поиграть в дурачки!»[54]

Тут поднялась в воздух, закружилась и вихрем налетела на Соню вся колода карт. С испуга и с досады Соня вскрикнула, замахнулась на неё… Ах!.. что такое? Где она?.. Лежит на траве, головой на коленях у сестры. Сестра осторожно смахивает ей с лица упавшие с дерева сухие листья.

«Проснись, Соничка!» тихо говорит сестра, «успокойся! ты, верно, сон видела. Уж очень ты заспалась, душенька!»

«Ах, Катя! что за удивительный приснился мне сон!» И Соня, как умела, пересказала сестре только что прочитанные вами странные приключения свои в царстве дива.

Notes

1 p. 7: *вёрст* / *vërst*. An old Russian unit of distance, a *verst* (Russ. *versta*) equaled 1.0668 km (0.6629 miles); thus 4,000 versts is only 2,651 miles. The radius of Earth being 3,959 miles, Carroll's Alice is, in fact, rather precise when she says 4,000 miles. However, Sonia is off by 33% since the translator did not adjust the number to fit real geography. There are some other discrepancies in units of distance and length between *Sonia* and Carroll's *Wonderland*. See Notes 4, 20, 21, 30, and 53 below.

2 p. 7: «Антипатия, *кажется, это место называется…*» / "Antipatiia, *kazhetsia, éto mesto nazyvaetsia* ("This place is called *Anthipathies*, I think…"'). Sonia thinks that the *country* is called Antipatia, akin to the English toponym Antipodes; a clever geographic pun, which works as well as Carroll's where Alice talks about the inhabitants of the country ("The antipathies, I think…").

3 p. 7: *Катюша* / *Katiusha* (also *Katiushka*) (or Katia, diminutive of Ekaterina). Stands for Dinah; also appears in the parody song replacing "*Father William*" (p. 39). It also happens to be the name of Sonia's sister (*Катя* / *Katia*) in the end of the story (p. 94)—the sister is nameless in Carroll's book. A nameless

female cat is also featured already in the parody poem that replaced "*How doth a little crocodile*" (p. 15).

A female cat is rare in Russian folklore, and has no fixed name, unlike a male cat, who is usually a Vasily, or Kotofey Ivanovich; there is also a magic cat Baiun ('a storyteller'), also a male. Note that the Cheshire-Cat becomes a female in *Sonia*, an unjustified change. While Dinah is clearly a female (and addressed as "she"), Cheshire-Cat is always "it"; however, Alice addresses it as a "Cheshire-Puss". It surely behaves as a male cat.

There is no Russian tradition to call female cats *Katia*. Could it be that a prominent presence of this added name in the text is the translator's own playful signature? See also Note 18.

4 p. 9: *вершок / vershok*. An old Russian unit of length, which equaled 4.4 cm (1.76 inches). Again, the translator did not adjust the numbers, and the little door, which measured a good 15 inches (37.5 cm) in Carroll's book, in *Sonia*'s case shrinks to only four vershoks, or 17.6 cm (7 inches).

5 p. 10: This illustration was not included in *Sonia*'s original edition; as is normal in Evertype's Carrollian books, the English label "DRINK ME" has been replaced by its Russian equivalent "ВЫПЕЙ МЕНЯ!».

6 p. 15: *«Киска хитрая не знает..."» /"Kiska khitraiia ne znaet…* " (' "A sly pussycat has not…" ')– this first parody poem that in *Sonia* replaces "*How doth the little crocodile*" refers to a standard text learned by all Russian schoolchildren, the first lines of Pushkin's *Цыганы* (*Tsygany*, '*The Gypsies*, 1824):

> «Птичка Божия не знает
> Ни заботы, ни труда,
> Хлопотливо не свивает
> Долговечного гнезда…»

> ("God's little bird has not
> Any care, any labour,
> It is not busy building
> A long-lasting nest…")

(Fan Parker erroneously translated "little bird" as "ladybird"; see reference on p. xi.) The parody is rendered in a childish verse but with a considerable skill in poetic parody; the translator follows the phonetics of the original Pushkin's lines with a truly Carrollian precision (*dolgovechnago gnezda* [a long-lasting nest] / *dlinnokhvostago zverka* [a long-tailed critter]).

One has an impression that the first translator received some assistance from a native English person who explained what the parody is about; how otherwise would s/he know that this verse parodies "*How doth a little busy bee…*"? We take it for granted now because we have Martin Gardner, Nina Demurova, and others who interpreted the *Wonderland* for us for 150 years—but none of this was available in Moscow of 1878! The same popular poem of Pushkin was used by other *Wonderland* translators: Matilda Granström in 1908; Poliksena Solovyova (pen name Allegro) in 1909; Vladimir Nabokov in 1923; and D'Aktil′ (pen name of Anatoly Frenkel′), also in 1923.

7 p. 18: *наш староста / nash starosta* – 'our village headman' (an elected position since the Russian reforms of 1861). In *Sonia*'s context, the word would indicate a village setting since she says 'next to our house' (*u nas okolo doma*). While Sonia is clearly an educated middle-class city child (who can even play a croquet game), in summer she could visit her parents' country estate, and thus could refer to 'our village headman' (in Carroll's original, the dog 'belongs to a farmer'). It is one of the markers of Sonia's social position, somewhat different from Alice's; see also a remarkable addition on p. 47 (see Note 24).

8 p. 19, 22, etc.: *Журавль / Zhuravl′* ('Crane', likely Common Crane, *Grus grus*). In *Sonia*, a Crane replaces the Dodo; later, cranes also replace unfamiliar flamingos as croquet mallets. Cranes are symbolic birds in Russian tradition: The departure of migratory cranes, in a typical wedge formation (*zhuravlinyi klin*), is an important mark of the coming fall in Russia; conversely, their arrival from the south designates the start of the spring. Cranes are sometimes represented in Russian

folklore and literary tales, e.g., *Лиса и журавль / Lisa i zhuravl'* ('A Fox and a Crane', where a Crane outsmarts a Fox by offering food from a tall pitcher that only the bird's beak can reach into). Following the word's grammatical gender, the crane is always *a male* figure, e.g., in the fairytale *Журавль и цапля / Zhuravl' i tsaplya* ('A Crane and a Heron') where the two plan to marry (heron being grammatically a female). Among Russian literary sources well-known to *Sonia*'s readers were Krylov's fable *Лягушки, просящие Царя / Liagushki, prosiashchie Tsaria* ('Frogs Asking for a Tsar', 1809, where Jupiter sends a Crane to be the Tsar of the Frogs; based on La Fontaine and Aesop fables), as well as Zhukovsky's classical ballad *Ивиковы журавли / Ivikovy zhuravli* ('The Cranes of Ivik', 1813), a free translation of Friedrich Schiller's *Die Kraniche des Ibykus*, 1797). Two Russian folk songs about cranes, *Журавль / Zhuravl'* and *Жур-Журавель / Zhur-Zhuravel'* can be found on pp. 35-36 and 56-57, respectively, of Mamontova & Solovyova's collection of children's games and songs published by *Sonia*'s publisher in 1872 (see footnote 36 on pp. xxi-xxii).

Cranes feed on frogs; thus inclusion of both species into a Pool of Tears crowd could be seen as a fairytale case of "a lion and a lamb"'s peaceful coexistence. The drawings of a crane replacing the Dodo (pp. 21, 23) and a flamingo (p. 70) have been kindly rendered for this edition by Byron W. Sewell.

9 p. 20: *горелки / gorelki* – 'tag', a game of chase today played only by children. The word is somewhat outdated, as well as its synonym, *салки / salki*, or *салочки / salochki*. Today, it is usually called *догоняшки / dogoniashki*. Originally, it was a pre-Christian game played by maidens and unmarried young men; a man was chasing a girl. A non-children's game of *gorelki* by young servants in a party is mentioned in Pushkin's *Барышня-Крестьянка / Baryshnia-Krest'ianka* ('Mistress into Maid', 1831).

10 p. 20: *глядят сентябрём / gliadiat sentiabrём* ('had a September look') – an old-fashioned poetic cliché meaning 'to look grim'. Here, most likely borrowed from the classical poetry

of the early nineteenth century (it is found in Derzhavin and Karamzin); used by Pushkin and Nikolai Yazykov as a political pun, "*no August smotrit sentiabrëm*" ("but August [possibly the Tsar Alexander I] looks like a September"); for a detailed discussion see: Лекманов, О. "Об одном пушкинском каламбуре" / Lekmanov, O. "Ob odnom pushkinskom kalambure" / '"On a pun by Pushkin"'), in *Пушкинские чтения в Тарту 4: Пушкинская эпоха: Проблемы рефлексии и комментария: Материалы международной конференции / Pushkinskie chteniia v Tartu 4. Pushkinskaia épokha: problemy refleksii i kommentariia* ('Pushkin Readings in Tartu 4: The Pushkin Epoch: The Problems of Reflection and Commentary'), Тарту / Tartu: Ülikooli Kirjastus, 2007, pp. 47–53; in Russian).

11 p. 22: *«Я в то время жила во дворце»* (*"Ia v to vremia zhila vo dvortse"*/ '"I lived at that time in a palace"') – Which palace what that? Within his single month of Moscow occupation (September—October 1812), Napoleon I mainly stayed in the Kremlin, in the quarters of the Tsar Alexander I, located in the old royal palace.

However, another possible palace is the Petrovskiy 'Way' Palace (Петровский путевой дворец), now within city limits. It was used by the Russian Tsars as a way station before entering Moscow on their way from St. Petersburg for the traditional coronation ceremony. Here, Napoleon stayed briefly during the great fire of Moscow (4–6 September 1812, Old Style) that the Mouse talks about.

Sonia's readers would immediately recall Pushkin's (1828) famous words about Napoleon and Petrovskiy Palace (*Eugene Onegin*: Canto Seven: XXXVII; transl. by Vladimir Nabokov):

Here is, surrounded by its park,
Petrovskiy castle. Somberly
it prides itself on recent glory.
In vain Napoleon, intoxicated
with his last fortune, waited
for kneeling Moscow with the keys

of old Kremlin; no,
to him my Moscow did not go
with craven brow;
not revelry, not gifts of *bienvenue*—
a conflagration she prepared
for the impatient hero.
From here, in meditation sunk,
He watched the formidable flame.

On the fire of Moscow, which almost completely destroyed the city, the Mouse says "*кто поджёг, неизвестно. Русские говорят на французов, французы сваливают на русских*"/ "*kto podzhëg, neizvestno. Russkie govoriat na frantsuzov, frantsuzy svalivaiut na Russkikh*" ('"Who started the fire, was unknown. Russians say it were the French, the French blame the Russians."'). In fact, there still is no consensus on the causes; today, most historians agree that at least the initial fires were due to Russian sabotage, as claimed already by the Napoleon's General Armand de Caulaincourt in 1812. The ambiguous Mouse, however, is more true to Lev Tolstoy, who suggests, in *War and Peace*, that the fire was not deliberately set, either by the Russians or the French, but was the natural result of placing a deserted and mostly wooden city in the hands of invading troops.

The Mouse's history lecture in *Sonia* is not really *dry*, but in fact quite lively. It also gives a definite impression not of a schoolteacher, as in Carroll, but of a schoolchild reciting a history lesson. Demurova (in "Sonja and Napoleon"), stated, incorrectly, that the translator (that is, the Mouse) describes the battle of Borodino (p. 21 in this volume) as a victory for the Russian army. It is not so: the Mouse, being French, brags about Napoleon's victory, saying "*Сразились под Бородиным, одержали победу*" / "*Srazilis' pod Borodinym, oderzhali pobedu*" ('"[We] fought the battle of Borodino, and won."'). For Russia, this battle (7 September 1812; 26 August, Old Style) was the turning point of the war; it was also the deadliest battle of Napoleonic Wars. The battle was indeed won by

Napoleon who captured Moscow, for only one month, on September 14. His victory, however, proved to be pyrrhic, so in Russian mentality until this day Borodino stands as a moral victory. It is featured in detail in Tolstoy's War and Peace, but it was also the subject of Mikhail Lermontov's patriotic poem *Бородино / Borodino* (1837), still a standard poem learned in Russian schools. In its famous first lines, a young man asks his uncle, an old Russian soldier: *"Скажи-ка, дядя, ведь недаром / Москва, спалённая пожаром, / Французу отдана?" / Skazhi-ka, diadia, ved' nedarom / Moskva, spalënnaia pozharom, / Frantsuzu otdana?"* ('"Tell me, uncle, was it not in vain, / That Moscow, burned by the fire, / Was surrendered to the French?"'). This Lermontov's poem was parodied in lieu of "*Father William*" in Vladimir Nabokov's *Wonderland* translation (1923), in which the Mouse also arrived to Russia with Napoleon. (Nabokov's Mouse's lecture, however, refers to the medieval Russian (Kievan Rus) history, and is rather dry compared to *Sonia*'s; its text was copied verbatim from a standard pre-revolutionary school textbook by Sergey Platonov.)

The Mouse says that she lived in *фургон с провиантом / furgon s proviantom* ('a supply wagon') and, at the same time, in a French soldier's *ранец / ranets* ('backpack'; Fan Parker erroneously called it a "Frenchman's briefcase"; see reference on p. xi, this volume). Technically, these are two different locations, unless the backpack belonged to the wagon's driver—but the Mouse would be comfortable in both. At the time of the Napoleonic invasion of Russia in 1812, the Grande Armée had 680,000 men (more than half of them perished by the time of retreat). "An army is a creature which marches on its stomach," said Napoleon; and each soldier carried four days' provisions in his backpack. The supply wagon trains following them carried mainly flour, thus the Mouse would face no shortage. Also, "living off the land" was encouraged. There is a famous scene in *War and Peace* (3: IV) of marauding French soldiers in Smolensk, filling their sacks and backpacks with wheat flour and sunflower seeds from a grocery store of the merchant Ferapontov—who, on seeing this, sets fire to his own store. *Sonia*'s readers would recognize the literary reference.

12 p. 24: *Громило / Gromilo*, from *grom*, 'thunder' – a dog's name, stands for Fury in the Mouse's Tale. Carroll's Fury is ambivalent, it could be either dog or cat; many modern translators choose a cat. Gromilo is a name for a male Russian hound (*vyzhlets*), listed in the notebooks of Nikolai Gogol′ (1841–1842); it appears in the list of Russian hounds of the 18th century.

13 p. 27: *Червонная Краля / Chervonnaia Kralia* ('The Queen of Hearts') replaces the Duchess here, and rightly so; it was an error on Lewis Carroll's part caused by imperfect editing of *Alice's Adventures under Ground*, the prototype of *Wonderland*. (Goodacre, Selwyn. *Elucidating Alice*, Evertype, 2015, footnotes 107 and 198). The translator was diligent enough to notice and correct the error. See also p. xxviii above.

14 p. 27: *Матрёна Ивановна / Matrëna Ivanovna*. Stands for Mary-Ann. A commoner's name (Sonia suggests she is the Rabbit's cook). Interestingly, Matrëna Ivanovna is one of the folk puppet theatre characters, a Petrushka's bride (a countryside girl who got city manners). Petrushka is a trickster puppet character known today mostly from Stravinsky's ballet (1910–1911) but traceable to the seventeenth century (Taruskin, R. *Stravinsky and the Russian Traditions, Volume One: A Biography of the Works*, Vol.1. UC Press, 1996). One such folk puppet play was recorded in northern Russia in 1896, with Matrëna Ivanovna being a Judy to this Russian Punch. Both characters appear in literary fairytales such as D. N. Mamin-Sibiriak's *Ванькины именины / Van'kiny imeniny* ('*Van'ka's Name Day*', 1897) and in a parody by Sasha Chërnyi *Петрушка в Париже / Petrushka v Parizhe* ('*Petrushka in Paris*', 1925). Adding a puppet character to scaled-down *Wonderland* folk is in accordance with translator's added imagery of Hatter's toy hat and (possibly) a miniature table croquet. None of Carroll's characters are, in fact, dolls or toys, but the translator creates more of a "Toyland" appearance.

15 pp. 27–28: *ДОМ ЦЕРЕМОНИЙМЕЙСТЕРА КРОЛИКОВСКОГО / DOM TSEREMONIIMEISTERA KROLIKOVSKOGO* 'The House of Marshal Krolikovsky' – this sign, comically long even in Russian (the title is derived from the German *Zeremonienmeister*), replaces Carroll's modest "W. RABBIT" sign. This archaic court position existed in Russia in 1879; it ranked in the 5th class (out of 12), equivalent to a State Councillor. *Krolikovsky* is a last name, here humorously derived from *krolik*, 'rabbit', but also existing in real life.

16 p. 30: *Петька/ Pet'ka* (diminutive of *Пётр / Pëtr*) is a rooster (*петух / petukh*, from *петь / pet'*, 'to sing, to crow'). Stands for Carroll's Pat (an unspecified creature). In Russian folklore, roosters are called *Pet'ka*. He is digging for *asparagus in a dung heap*; could be a reference to Ivan Krylov's fable *Петух и жемчужное зерно / Petukh i zhemchuzhnoe zerno* ('The Rooster and a Pearl', 1808), derived from La Fontaine's fable *Le Coq et la Perle* (1668). See also Note 17.

17 p. 30: *хохлатый тетерев / khokhlatyi teterev*. This added name—with which the White Rabbit addressed Pat instead of "you goose!"—is the most obscure expression in *Sonia*. Literally, it means a 'crested grouse' (shown below) but there is no such bird in Russia. 'Teterev' is the Black Grouse (*Lyrurus tetrix*), a well-known Russian game bird, but it is not in any way "crested"; and the combination hardly can be seen as a

The Pinnated Grouse: two males displaying their crests in the foreground, a female in the background. From: Forbush, Edward H. *Game Birds, Wild-Fowl and Shore Birds of Massachusetts and Adjacent States*. Massachusetts State Board of Agriculture, 1912.

nonsensical address. The exact combination *khokhlatyi teterev*, however, appears in English-Russian dictionaries contemporary with *Sonia* (e.g. Tauschnitz's pocket dictionary published in Leipzig in 1830s–1890s). There, it is listed as a Russian translation of "Heath-cock." In Europe, this name traditionally refers to the same Black Grouse. However, in North America, "Heath-cock" (or, more commonly "Heath-hen") at this time referred to the now-extinct Pinnated Grouse, or Great Prairie Chicken (*Tympanuchus cupido*), males of which had a distinct double set of feathery crests (hence, "pinnated").

However, why in the world would be Pat called a Pinnated Grouse in Russian? The only possible solution I can suggest is a rather complex charade. A reader is supposed to insert the English term for *khokhlatyi teterev* as a *Heath-hen*; to recognize a Carroll-style phonetic pun as *Heathen*; and to decode Rabbit's sentence as "*Arm, you heathen!*" This combination, in its turn, readdresses one to the famous scene from English classical literature, which is also full of puns.

Hamlet was read, translated many times, and staged in Russia widely by the 1870s. In its Act 5, Scene 1, we find the dialogue of two gravediggers:

GRAVEDIGGER

> [...] Come, my spade. There is no ancient gentleman but gardeners, ditchers, and grave-makers: they hold up Adam's profession.

OTHER

> Was he a gentleman?

GRAVEDIGGER

> He was the first that ever bore arms.

OTHER

> Why, he had none.

GRAVEDIGGER

> What, art a heathen? How dost thou understand the Scripture? The Scripture says Adam digged. Could he dig without arms?

Alice's *arm* ("arrum") is what the Rabbit and Pat (*'a heathen'*) are discussing. Pat, who in *Sonia* is a rooster (same bird family as *heath-hen*), *digs* with his feet, i.e. "*without arms*"; and he is also a *gardener*. Since Pat is a male, he is a heath-cock (*teterev*, masc.), not a heath-hen (*tetërka*, fem.). One can see such scenes discussed (and maybe even enacted) by Russians of the 1870s (such as the Timiryazev family) reading *Hamlet* and *Wonderland* in English; complex literary charades are still played in educated households.

The 'heath-hen/heathen' pun is found in at least one historical anecdote, published by the Scottish-American poet and ornithologist Alexander Wilson (1766–1813), the "Father of the American Ornithology." As early as 1791, a bill titled "An Act for the preservation of Heath-Hen, and other game" was introduced in the New York State legislature. Wilson wrote: "The honest Chairman of the Assembly—no sportsman, I suppose—read the title, '"An Act for the preservation of Heathen, and other game"!' which seemed to astonish the northern members, who could not see the propriety of preserving Indians, or any other heathens". This quote is found in *Wilson's American Ornithology*, where the species is called a "Pinnated Grouse", as early as 1829. I found the same story in an American children's magazine that matches *Sonia*'s translation timeframe (*Our Young Folks: An Illustrated Magazine for Boys and Girls*, Boston, Vol. 7, No 1, January 1871, p. 676–680: "Prairie-Chickens" by F. M. Gray). On p. 680, the anecdote is recounted, and on p. 676 one sees a nice image of a Pinnated Grouse. The story became known across the world since the New York 1791 act was one of the first ever to legislate wildlife protection. It is found even in modern Russian sources although today the extinct American species is called *vostochnyi stepnoi teterev* ("Eastern Steppe Grouse"), or *lugovoi teterev* ("Meadow Grouse").

Of course, it is entirely possible to arrive to the 'heath-hen/heathen' pun independently from the American ornithological anecdote. For example, Sir Walter Scott, who was very widely read in Russia—and whom Vasily Arkadyevich

Timiryazev, Ekaterina Boratynskaya's uncle, translated into Russian!—mentions both "heath-cock" and "heath-hen": "Fergus, all the while, with his myrmidons, striding stoutly by his side, or diverging to get a shot at a roe or a heath-cock." (*Waverley*, 1814, Ch. 24); "On yonder mountain's purple head / Have ptarmigan and heath-cock bled" (*The Lady of the Lake*, 1810, 1:22); "... she would sit still as a heath-hen when the hawk is in the heavens." (*Anne of Geierstein, or The Maiden of the Mist*, 1829, Ch. 36). In these cases, however, the bird is the European Black Grouse. Thus a translator would have to apply the imprecise dictionary entry 'khokhlatyi teterev' (Pinnated Grouse), which refers only to the American species.

Whatever is the origin of this pun, in *Sonia*'s text it appears very incongruent since it is not decoded: a Russian reader would not know what to make of *khokhlatyi teterev* without a back-translation into English. I suggest that this unexplained riddle is a possible trace of a domestic charade (played by *Sonia*'s translator or in her household), which was not properly explained or edited in the published text. The same refers to the enigmatic, endearing *Gneden'kaia* ("Litle Bay") name, with which Iliushka (the Hatter) addresses Sonia (see Note 33), and possibly also to the strange boarded croquet ground (see Note 42). These incongruent additions, as well as truncated last two chapters, seem to indicate an unfinished nature of *Sonia*'s text, which initially (and/or partially) might have been intended for a narrow, domestic audience.

18 p. 31: *Васька / Vas'ka* (diminutive of *Василий / Vasily*) is a cockroach, standing in for Carroll's Bill the Lizard. It is also called a "blackamoore" (*черномазый / chernomazyi*, p. 33; *черномазенький / chernomazen'kii*, p. 90), which indicates a large black Oriental cockroach (*Blatta orientalis*) rather than a small, red German cockroach *Blattella germanica*—both being scourges of a Russian kitchen. Vas'ka is a random male name for a cockroach, not found in folklore, where Vas'ka in fact is commonly a male *cat's* name. (Dinah becomes a *male* Vas'ka in Matilda Granstrem's translation of 1908!) The drawing of this

character (on pp. 32 and 91) has been rendered for this edition by Byron W. Sewell and Michael Everson.

Cockroaches are not prominent in Russian folklore, although later (and probably independent of *Sonia*) a cockroach becomes an evil dictatorial figure in Korney Chukovsky's popular children's poem *Тараканище / Tarakanishche* ('A Big Cockroach', 1921).

There is no reason why a cockroach would be called either *Vas'ka* or *Vasily*. One wonders if this isn't another playful domestic reference, along with *Katia* (Ekaterina) present prominently in the text. Ekaterina Boratynskaya had a younger brother, Vasily Ivanovich Timiryazev (1849–1919), who grew up to be the first Russian Minister of Trade.

19 p. 38: *„Близко города Славянска…" („Blizko goroda Slavianska…" / „Near the town of Slaviansk…").* Instead of "*Father William*", Sonia recites a large, original parody of a very popular aria from an early Russian opera, *Askol'dova mogila* (*The Askold's Tomb*) by Verstovsky (1835; libretto by Zagoskin). See "Sonia's Adventures" (above, p. xxvii) for further comments.

20 p. 40: The Caterpillar's size equals two vershoks (8.8 cm, or 3.52 inches), which is just slightly more than Carroll's three inches.

21 p. 44: *Аршин / arshin*; *полуаршина / poluarshina:* 'half-arshin'. *Arshin* is another old Russian unit of length, which equaled 71.12 cm (28 inches). The arshin-sized Duchess's house in *Sonia* is almost two times smaller than in *Alice* (four feet, or 48 inches). To enter this house, Carroll's Alice adjusts her size to *nine* inches (19% of the house's height) while Sonia, incongruously, adjusts her size to *a half* of house's height (*poluarshin*, or 14 inches). The translator might have taken a clue from the Tenniel picture, which implies that the Duchess's kitchen ceiling is quite low.

22 p. 45: *«Пиковой Княгине приглашение от Червонной Крали» ("Pikovoy Kniagine priglashenie ot Chervonnoy Krali"* / "An invitation to the Princess of Spades [the Duchess] from the Queen of Hearts"). See "Sonia's Adventures" (above, p. xxviii)

for explanations on the translation of the titles of these characters.

23 p. 45: There is a footnote here (p. 72 of the original), explaining the word *kroket* 'croquet' as *igra v shary, vrode lugovogo bil'iarda* ('a ball game, a kind of lawn billiard'. The footnote of course is absent in Lewis Carroll's *Wonderland*. It contradicts the description of a board-paved croquet ground in *Sonia*, which could refer to a miniature table croquet (see Note 42). This footnote (the only one in the book) could belong not to the translator but to another person.

24 p. 47: *«Ни на что не похоже!» ворчит она, «как эти люди нынче стали рассуждать! не сладишь с ними: совсем из повиновенья вышли!» / "Ni na chto ne pokhozhe!" vorchit ona, "kak éti liudi nynche stali rassuzhdat'! Ne sladish' s nimi: sovsem iz povinoven'ia vyshli!"* ("What is all that?" she complained, "the way these people are talking now! One can't cope with them: they've completely lost all obedience!") – None of this is found in Lewis Carroll. In the context of post-1861 reforms in Russia, the words are meant as an irony. Sonia clearly repeats the complaints she has heard from the adults about the unruly behaviour of the lower classes (the Frog-Footman).

25 The Frog-Footman, instead of saying "I will sit here... for days and days," uses the Orthodox Christian formula *"i nyne i zavtra i vo veki vekov"* ('today and forever and unto ages and ages', Lat. "et nunc et semper et saecula saeculorum" / Gr. "εἰς τοὺς αἰῶνας τῶν αἰώνων" / "eis toùs aiõnas tõn aiónōn"). The formula if found in many prayers, the shortest being a 16-word Trisviatoe (Holy Trinity Prayer): "*Слава Отцу и Сыну и Святому Духу и ныне и присно и во веки веков. Аминь."/ "Slava Otsu i Synu i Sviatomu Dukhu i nyne i prisno i vo veki vekov. Amin'"* ('Glory be to the Father, and to the Son and to the Holy Spirit today, and forever, and for ages and ages'). Trisviatoe must be read in the beginning of every service, at home or at church. It is the most common Orthodox prayer, which corresponds to Gloria Patri ("the Glory Be") also known as the Lesser Doxology. In

the Anglican version, the words "saecula saeculorum" were translated in the 16th century as "world without end."

Sonia refers to the Frog-Footman on the same page as to a low-class servant whose education would be limited to a Sunday school (Church parish school, or *tserkovnoprikhodskaiia shkola*). It was common in the 1870s Russia to hear low-class people's speech peppered by liturgical formulae. The translator intentionally makes the Frog-Footman to sound even more pompous than in Carroll's text, which in Russian is easily achieved by using a standard Church Slavonic formula.

The Footman is also illiterate: it incorrectly uses 19th-century Russian *завтра / zavtra* ('tomorrow') instead of Church Slavonic *присно / prisno* ('forever'). This is easily detected by a child reader. The Bible translation from the Church Slavonic into modern Russian was a hot issue in 1879: the first full translation was only published in 1876. The very permission to translate the Bible (1868) was a part of the sweeping social reforms by Alexander II, which surround the 1879 edition and percolate to its children readers in many points.

26 p. 49: *Сибирская Кошка, Киска* (*Sibirskaia Koshka, Kiska / Siberian Cat, Pussycat*). The Cheshire-Cat, which is a female (*koshka*) in *Sonia*. *Kiska* ('pussycat') is an endearing/childish word. "Siberian" does not imply any negative meaning; it is just a big, fluffy domestic cat of an aboriginal Russian breed, possibly related to Persian cats. (In fact, Fan Parker erroneously called the *Sonia* character a Persian Cat; see the reference on p. xi above.) In all modern Russian translations the Cheshire-Cat is a male (*kot*), usually rendered simply as a Cheshirskii Kot. A Siberian male cat is found in Afanasyev's fairytales, named Kotofey Ivanovich; in other folkloric sources the cat's breed is not specified. The cat theme is enhanced in *Sonia* compared to *Alice*; see Notes 3 and 6.

27 p. 50: The last line of the Duchess's song is replaced in the 1879 edition (p. 83 in the original) by a strange line of dots; Sergey Kuriy suggested that the line was removed by a censor. It is

impossible to guess what the line was; it would rhyme with many Russian verbs. The poem is a *double* parody, based on a widely known Mikhail Lermontov's *Казачья колыбельная* / *Kazach'ia kolybel'naia* (*'The Cossack Lullaby'*, 1840), and *also* on its caustic political parody, Nikolai Nekrasov's *Колыбельная песня* / *Kolybel'naia pesnia* (*'The Lullaby'*, 1845).

28 p. 53: *Враль-Илюшка / Vral'-Iliushka ('Iliushka the Liar').* An invented name, not found in Russian folklore. The name Iliushka (diminutive of Ilya) does not imply any specific features, although it appears to designate a low-class person. Demurova (2013) assumed that it has a humorous form, which is not necessarily so. It is not clear how Iliushka is a 'Liar' (of a 'Fibber') although this might mean that his story about Time in the Mad Tea-Party chapter is just a fib. He is further called Vral' only once, on p. 87.

29 p. 53: *Заяц Косой / Zaiats Kosoi* ('The Cross-eyed Hare'), later called only the Hare. The standard epithet 'Cross-eyed', often as a stand-alone name, is commonly used in Russian folklore for a hare (a standard folkloric character, as opposed to a rabbit, which is foreign for Russia). It does not imply strong negative meaning in folklore; however, *окосеть / okoset'* ('to become cross-eyed') has a second meaning 'to become mad', and thus could be seen as the translator's attempt to indicate madness. The folksy word *Sonia*'s translator used for 'mad' is *шальной / shal'noi*, and the derived verb *ошалеть / oshalet'* is a synonym of *okoset'*.

30 p. 55: Before she enters the Hare's house, Sonia's size becomes a full arshin (28 inches), slightly higher than Alice, who rises to two feet (24 inches).

31 p. 56: In *Sonia*, the Mad Tea-Party table is set in a room *inside* the Hare's house, clearly contradicting Carroll's text (where it is set "under a tree in front of the house") as well as Tenniel's picture reproduced on p. 95 of the 1879 edition (p. 57 here).

32 p. 56: *Мишенька-Сурок / Mishen'ka-Surok* ('Mishen'ka the Marmot') is an unusual choice, but the translator obviously could not use the Russian word for a 'dormouse' (*соня /sonia*), which

is a full homophone of the name *Соня / Sonia*. Marmots (or woodchucks, genus *Marmota*) are much larger in size (50–70 cm) than dormice. They are found in southern European Russian grasslands (steppes) but are not very familiar animals to a Russian child. There is, however, a common saying *спит, как сурок / spit, kak surok* 'sleeps as a marmot', which perfectly fits the Mad Tea-Party's sleepy animal. Another cultural reference is the famous Beethoven song *Marmotte* (1805), based on Goethe's lyrics (1774), "*Ich komme schon durch manches Land avecque la marmotte...*") and highly popular in Russia. The song was commonly played by wandering organ players. It was, and remains, a standard piece in children's music lessons. Also widely known was a painting by Antoine Watteau, *Savoyard with a Marmot* (1715), housed in the Hermitage Museum, St. Petersburg (purchased for Catherine the Great between 1774 and 1797), probably the most famous marmot painting. Watteau's marmot is almost a size of Tenniel's Dormouse, which is larger than a real dormouse. (Lore has it that the animal was based on Dante Gabriel Rossetti's pet wombat, which is a size of a marmot or larger.)

Marmots do not have a Russian folklore name; however, *Мишенька / Mishen'ka* (or Mishka, both diminutives of Michael) is a standard folklore name for a brown bear. It is clear that giving a nameless Dormouse a proper name was intended to make the image closer to Russian folklore. Since bears are also known to hibernate, an impression the translator creates is of a sleepy animal resembling a small bear, or a bear cub. It is very typical for *Sonia*'s translator to experiment with such cross-cultural hybridization, often creating eclectic imagery. A Marmot also replaced the Dormouse in other early Russian translations by Matilda Granström (1908) and Alexandra Rozhdestvenskaya (1908–1909).

33 p. 57, 59: *Гнеденькая* (*Gneden'kaia*, 'A Little Bay', from *gnedaia*, 'bay' [horse]). This rather strange addition is a female horse's name, with which Iliushka (the Hatter) addresses Sonia, who indignantly replies: "There are no such names!" The name

is followed by *vam ne meshalo by postrich' grivku* ('you should cut your little mane' for 'your hair wants cutting'), referring to Sonia's hair as an equine mane (Russ. *griva*, also used for long human hair). Both *gneden'kaia* and *grivka* are rather endearing words. The word *gneden'kaia* is found in one of Lev Tolstoy's early stories, *Метель / Metel'* ('A Snowstorm,' 1856), which would have been a commonly-read text in the 1870s. This could be also a hint about the added phonetic pun on the Jurors (see Note 51 to p. 86) since in Tolstoy's story the little bay is a *pristiazhnaia*, a side horse in a *troika*. The same story has a central character called Ignashka, which sounds close to Iliushka. Morover, another 1856 story by Tolstoy, *Два гусара / Dva gusara* 'Two Hussars') has a Gypsy character called Iliushka. The *Gneden'kaia* addition, which is not explained to the reader, could be a trace of a domestic charade/parody if *Sonia* text was insufficiently edited (see p. xxx above).

34 p. 57 and 87, drawings: in *Sonia*'s original edition, the price label of the Hatter's hat (Tenniel's "10/6") was replaced with «*50 коп.*[*еек*]» ('50 kopecks'); this is reproduced here. See "Sonia's Adventures" (above, p. xxx) for further comments. Such a "scaled" price could correspond to a *toy* hat, just like the changed description of croquet ground as a possible miniature parlour game (see Note 42).

35 p. 58: *«И прибрал же себе» / «I pribral zhe sebe» – прибрать себе / pribrat' sebe* is an outdated expression meaning 'to take over, to grab'. The sentence is obscure; possibly, Iliushka means that Mishen'ka jumped in the conversation just in time (*kak raz kstati*).

36 p. 59: *«Ты, видно, не пряха, не ткаха!» / "Ty, vidno, ne priakha, ne tkakha!"* ("One can see that you are neither a spinstress nor a weaver!»)–an archaic folk saying; Iliushka implies that Sonia is not very skilled in solving riddles. Another example of an added folkloric expression to make the text sound more like a Russian tale. *Tkakha* is a folksy contraction of *tkachikha*. Both are common female occupations in many a folklore and literary tales.

This expression is mostly known from the Russian proverb "*Ни ткаха, ни пряха, а язык, как плаха / Ni tkakha, ni priakha, a iazyk, kak plakha* ('Neither a weaver, nor a spinstress, but [her] tongue is like a chopping block'). More importantly, the same formula is also found in an archaic folk game *Просо / Proso* ('The Millet') played by maidens. There, words "*она у нас дурочка, не пряха, не ткаха / ona u nas durochka, ne priakha, ne tkakha* ('she is a fool, neither a spinstress nor a weaver') are applied to a newcomer, an uninitiated maiden who should be taught the rules of the game; this fits Sonia's role at the Mad Tea-Party table. In another similar game, *Лён / Lën* ("The Flax'), girls split into teams of spinstresses (*priakhi*) and weavers (*tkakhi*). (Бернштам, Т. А. "Совершеннолетние девушки в метафорах игрового фольклора (традиционный аспект русской культуры)". В кн.: Байбурин, А. К., Кон, И. С. (ред.). *Этнические стереотипы мужского и женского поведения*. С.-Петербург: Наука, 1991, с. 233–256 / Bernshtam, T. A. "Sovershennoletnie devushki v metaforakh igrovogo fol′klora (traditsionnyi aspect russkoi kul′tury" 'Adult maidens in the metaphors of game folklore (a traditional aspect of Russian culture)'". In: Bayburin, A. K. and Kon, I. S. (eds.). *Étnicheskie stereotipy muzhskogo i zhenskogo povedeniia* 'The Ethnic Stereotypes of Male and Female Behavior'). St. Petersburg: Nauka, 1991, pp. 233–256; in Russian).

The text and score of two folk songs accompanying both *Lën* and *Proso* games can be found on pp. 15–16 and 52–53, respectively, of Mamontova & Solovyova's collection of children's games and songs, published by *Sonia*'s publisher Anatoly Mamontov in 1872 (see "Sonia's Adventures", this volume, footnote 36 on pp. xxi-xxii). This *Proso* version did not include "*не пряха, не ткаха*" formula; however, the *Lën* song includes traditional lines sung by the maidens referring to spinning and weaving: "*Уж я пряла, я пряла ленок... Уж я ткала, я ткала мой холст...*"/ "*Uzh ia priala, ia priala lenok… Uzh ia tkala, ia tkala moy kholst…*" 'So was I spinning and spinning my flax… So was I weaving and weaving my cloth…').

37 p. 61: Here, Iliushka (the Hatter) and Zaiats (the Hare) address Mishen′ka (the Dormouse) as Соня (Sonia)! (*Эй, Соня, будет тебе спать! / Éi, Sonia, budet tebe spat′!* 'Wake up, Dormouse!') In this phrase, 'sonia' is intended as a 'sleepy-head' and should have not be capitalized, which was clearly a printer's error. In addition to being a girl's name, *соня* (*sonia*) in Russian means both 'a sleepy-head' and 'dormouse'.

38 p. 61: *под ключом / pod kliuchom*, literally, 'under a key', has a double meaning of living next to a water source, and in a locked house (room); both expressions are obsolete today, although the same pun was used by Alexander Shcherbakov (1977) in his translation of *Wonderland*.

39 p. 61: *дрёма / drëma* (or *dremota*) means 'light sleep' and also is a name of a common Russian flower, either white campion (*Silene latifolia*, or *S. alba*) or clammy campion, *lipkaiia drëma* (*Viscaria vulgaris*, or *Lychnis viscaria*), both of the carnation family (Caryophyllaceae). The treacle-well girls are *eating* campion and becoming "very sick"; Russian ethnobotany maintains that campion has a somniferous effect; in folklore, it is also called *son-trava* ('sleeping herb'). An additional pun used in this text connects дрёма to a folkloric expression *в дремучем лесу / v dremuchem lesu* ('in the thick forest') where the treacle-well girls lived.

A cultural reference, which would be known to *Sonia*'s readers, is *drëma* in Alexander Ostrovsky's fairytale play *Снегурочка / Snegurochka* ('Snow Maiden', 1873; first staged in Moscow, 1873). The play was based on Afanasyev's fundamental work *Поэтические воззрения славян на природу / Poéticheskie vozzreniia slavian na prirodu* ('Poetic Views on the Nature of the Slavs', 1865–1869). In Ostrovsky's play, *lipkaiia drëma* is one of the nine flowers in the Snow Maiden's magic "spring wreath" (a gift from her mother, Spring, which leads to Snow Maiden's demise.) See: Шарафадина, К. И. "Флористическая «загадка» А. Н. Островского, или этноботаническая интерпретация «венка весны для Снегурочки»", in *Этноботаника: растения в языке и культуре*. СПб.: Наука, 2010,

c. 164–189. / Sharafadina, K. I. "Floristicheskaiia 'zagadka' A.N. Ostrovskogo, ili étnobotanicheskaia interpretatsiia 'venka vesny dlia Snegurochki'", in *Étnobotanika: rasteniia v iazyke i kul'ture.* ("'A floristic 'riddle' of A. N. Ostrovsky, or an ethnobotanical interpretation of the 'spring wreath for Snegurochka'", in *Ethnobotany: Plants in Language and Culture.*) St. Petersburg: Nauka, 2010, pp. 164–189, in Russian).

On 6 January 1882, *Snegurochka* was staged in the domestic theatre of Savva Mamontov, enacted by the Mamontov family members (including *Sonia*'s publisher's daughter, Tatiana) and friends, including famous artists such as Repin and Vasnetsov; Vasnetsov also designed set and costumes (on the Mamontovs, see "Sonia's Adventures", above, pp. xx-xxii). In 1885, Mamontov staged Nikolay Rimsky-Korsakov's opera *Snegurochka* (1881, first staged 1882), based on the same play, in Vasnetsov's designs.

40 p. 61: *хворость … хворостом выбивали* / *khvorost' … khvorostom vybivali* ('the illness was beaten out with firewood'), a very clever, truly Carrollian phonetic pun. It is based on a one-letter (the terminal soft sign, ь) and one-sound difference between *khvorost'* (illness) and *khvorost* (firewood). Moreover, before the 1918 orthographic reform, the latter word was written with a terminal hard sign (ъ), and thus for Sonia's readers, the visual difference appeared to be less than one letter (ъ versus ь).

41 p. 67: *фофаны* / *fofany* – (the *Sonia* text had, incorrectly, *fofony*), 'fools, dunces'; an outdated word, also an obsolete synonym for a simple card game of 'fools' (*дураки/duraki, дурачки/durachki*). The latter is mentioned in the last chapter, p. 93. The word *fofan* is derived from the Russian name Feofan (Greek 'Theophane').

42 p. 69: *Площадка вся неровная: где доска гнилая, где торчит ребром, а где вовсе провалилась* / *Ploshchadka vsia nerovnaia: gde doska gnilaia, gde torchit rebrom, a gde vovse provalilas'* ('The court was all uneven: here, a board is rotten; here, a board sticks out with its side; and here, one completely fell through'). This added description does not fit Carroll's croquet field with its

earthen 'ridges and furrows'. Thus, *Sonia*'s text describes a strange croquet court (*площадка / ploshchadka*), which is not an uneven lawn (as in *Wonderland*) but a sort of board-covered deck. It is possible that the translator described here a miniature table croquet (*настольный крокет / nastol'nyi kroket*), a parlour game familiar to *Sonia*'s readers. It nicely fits the scale of Wonderland characters. This game was popular in pre-revolutionary Russia and is still played there. See also Note 21.

43 p. 74: In this translation, Sonia does not hold her flamingo when she is approached by the Duchess; instead, she left her crane behind but kept the hedgehog, carrying it in her headscarf. Accordingly, the Duchess is afraid of the prickly hedgehog, not of a biting flamingo. The drawing of this scene has been rendered for this edition by Byron W. Sewell.

44 p. 77: *все они идут ко мне на кухню / vse oni idut ko mne na kukhniu* ('they all go to my kitchen'). The Queen leaves no doubt that the animals in her 'menagerie' are kept as food items! This discovery makes the Queen even more repulsive; mock turtle soup is bad enough, but it is hard to imagine an *edible* Gryphon. The royal kitchen is mentioned earlier in Carroll's book: the Seven, one of the gardeners, sent there tulip roots instead of onions (p. 64).

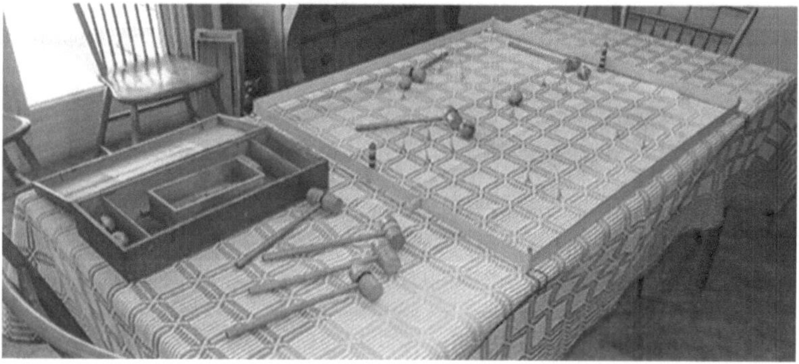

A vintage boxwood table croquet set, restored and photographed by Ernie Conover, http://www.woodworkersjournal.com/miniature-croquet-set-features-full-size-details/

45 p. 78: *Телячья Головка* / *Teliach'ia Golovka* ('Calf-Head'). This is how, based on Tenniel's illustrations, *Sonia*'s translator rendered the Mock Turtle. Mock turtle soup was well-known in Russia at that time under its French name, *fausse tortu*; a reader (at least a middle-class one) would know that this dish was made from a calf's head. See p. xxv above for more details.

46 p. 80: *«Мы его называли морем, потому что нас там морили»* / *"My ego nazyvali morem, potomu chto nas tam morili"* ('We called it a sea because we were starved there'). Most of the Mock Turtle's and Gryphon's phonetic puns were omitted by the translator, but a few very good ones are introduced. Here, the Calf-Head explains that he and other calves lived in a saltwater pool (*solënyi basseyn*) but they called this pool a sea (*more*) because the calves were *morili* (starved, tortured) there.

47 p. 80: *«... склонение, спряжение...»* ... *«слоняние, наряжание...»*. This is the reduced school pun; instead of four actions of arithmetic there are two terms from grammar. Sonia recalls *sklonenie* and *spriazhenie* ('declension' [of nouns] and 'conjugation' [of verbs]); the Calf-Head's pun says *slonianie* and *nariazhanie* ('loafing' and 'dressing-up').

48 p. 84: The four-line parody poem in *Sonia* that replaces "*'Tis the voice of the Lobster*" is rich in school references as well as freewheeling surrealism:

«Раз, собравшися в кружок,
Петухи гадали,
На ворота колпачок,
Сняв с ноги, сажали:»

("Once, gathered into a circle,
Roosters were telling fortunes,
They placed over the gate
A hood they took off their foot.")

Sonia's readers would immediately recognize this nonsensical quatrain as a parody of the first four lines of Vasily Zhukovsky's famous romantic ballad *Светлана / Svetlana* (1813):

«Раз в крещенский вечерок
Девушки гадали:
За ворота башмачок,
Сняв с ноги, бросали. »

("Once, on the twelfth day of Christmas
Maidens were telling fortunes,
They threw over the gate
A shoe they took off their foot.")

This is a descripton of maidens' midwinter ritual of *sviatochnye gadaniia*, divination for a bridegroom on the *kreshchenskii vecherok*, the Epiphany Eve (*Sviatki* is a twelve day-period between Christmas and the Epiphany). Zhukovsky's ballad was immensely popular and became a folk song; it also readdresses a reader to Pushkin's *Eugene Onegin*. There, Svetlana provides an epigraph to Canto Five ("Never know these frightful dreams, You, O my Svetlana!"), which features the most famous maiden's nightmare in Russian literature (*son Tat'iany* 'Tatiana's Dream'). A rooster-headed creature is one of the monsters in this Boschian dream (Canto Five: XVI: "She sees… at a table monsters are seated in a circle: one horned and dog-faced; another with a rooster's head"; transl. by V. Nabokov). In *Sonia*, Pat also becomes a rooster named Pet'ka. Generally, a rooster is an important Russian folkloric figure related to solar magic; its triple crowing repels the evil forces. Thus, the translator connects Sonia's peculiar dream to Tatyana's nightmare. Nabokov, in his commentary to *Eugene Onegin*, called Zhukovsky's ballad a "masterpiece" and suggested that it could have been a source of Pushkin's highly original "Onegin stanza."

49 p. 85: *«Ах, прекраснейший суп*
Из головки телячьей!..»

("Oh, a beautiful soup
Made of calf-head!")

This song, heavily abridged just to two lines, leaves no doubt that the Calf-Head is singing about a soup made of himself at Queen's kitchen. See also Note 44.

50 p. 86: Fan Parker noted that instead of a wig, Sonia identifies the judge by a chain on his breast. No such chain is present on Tenniel's illustration that was reproduced in *Sonia*.

51 p. 86: «Это, должно быть, пристяжные,» подумала Соня. Она, видите, говорила «пристяжные», потому что не совсем затвердила слово *присяжные*. ('"These are probably *pristiazhnye* [side horses]," thought Sonia. You see, she said *pristiazhnye* [side horses] because she did not quite know the word *prisiazhnye* [jurors].') *Pristiazhnye* are side horses in a Russian troika. See "Sonia's Adventures", above, p. xxvi.

52 p. 91: *«А вы, друзья, как ни садитесь,*
Всё в музыканты не годитесь!»

("And you, my friends, can change positions:
This will not make you good musicians")

These two lines are not a parody but a direct quote from Krylov's fable *Квартет / Kvartet* ('The Quartet' 1811). Already in the 1870s, this was a clichéd expression directed at an inept group of people (in the fable, animal musicians) who try to improve situation by exchanging their positions.

53 p. 91 *сажень / sazhen'*, an old Russian unit of length, 7 feet (2.133 m), which is nearly not as impressive than Carroll's *mile*. See also p. 13 where Sonia extends "almost to a sazhen'" (while Alice becomes more than nine feet high).

54 p. 93: *«Все-то вы колода карт и больше ничего—годны разве только поиграть в дурачки!» ("You are nothing but a pack of cards, good only to play 'fools'!)* – the last six words of *Sonia* are added by the translator. *Durachki*, or *duraki*, *durak*, 'fool(s)', is the simplest of Russian card games, still very widely played.

ALSO AVAILABLE FROM EVERTYPE

SOURCES

Alice's Adventures in Wonderland: The Evertype definitive edition,
by Lewis Carroll, 2016

Alice's Adventures in Wonderland, illus. June Lornie, 2013

Alice's Adventures in Wonderland, illus. Mathew Staunton, 2015

Alice's Adventures in Wonderland, illus. Harry Furniss, 2016

Through the Looking-Glass and What Alice Found There,
by Lewis Carroll, 2009

The Nursery "Alice", by Lewis Carroll, 2015

Alice's Adventures under Ground, by Lewis Carroll, 2009

The Hunting of the Snark, by Lewis Carroll, 2010

SEQUELS

A New Alice in the Old Wonderland, by Anna Matlack Richards, 2009

New Adventures of Alice, by John Rae, 2010

Alice Through the Needle's Eye, by Gilbert Adair, 2012

Wonderland Revisited and the Games Alice Played There,
by Keith Sheppard, 2009

Alice and the Boy who Slew the Jabberwock,
by Allan William Parkes, 2016

SPELLING

Alice's Adventures in Wonderland,
Retold in words of one Syllable by Mrs J. C. Gorham, 2010

𐐈𐑊𐐮𐑅'𐑆 𐐈𐐼𐑂𐐯𐑌𐐽𐐲𐑉𐑆 𐐮𐑌 𐐎𐐲𐑌𐐼𐐲𐑉𐑊𐐰𐑌𐐼,
Alice printed in the Deseret Alphabet, 2014

𐐜 𐐐𐐲𐑌𐐻𐐮𐑍 𐐲𐑂 𐑄 𐐝𐑌𐐪𐑉𐐿,
The Hunting of the Snark printed in the Deseret Alphabet, 2016

𐐛𐑉𐐭 𐑄 𐐢𐐳𐐿𐐮𐑍-𐐘𐑊𐐰𐑅 𐐰𐑌𐐼 𐐐𐐶𐐲𐐻 𐐈𐑊𐐮𐑅 𐐙𐐵𐑌𐐼 𐐜𐐯𐑉,
Looking-Glass printed in the Deseret Alphabet, 2016

Alice's Adventures in Wonderland,
Alice printed in Dyslexic-Friendly fonts, 2015

[illegible],
Alice printed in a font that simulates Dyslexia, 2015

[illegible],
Alice printed in the Ewellic Alphabet, 2013

'Ælɪsɪz Əd'ventʃəz ɪn 'Wʌndəˌlænd,
Alice printed in the International Phonetic Alphabet, 2014

Alis'z Advnčrz in Wunḍland, *Alice* printed in the Ñspel orthography, 2015

[illegible],
Alice printed in the Nyctographic Square Alphabet, 2011

[illegible], *Alice* printed in the Shaw Alphabet, 2013

ALISIZ ADVENCƎRZ IN WUNDЯLAND,
Alice printed in the Unifon Alphabet, 2014

[illegible] (Aliz kalandjai Csodaországban),
The Hungarian *Alice* printed in Old Hungarian script, tr. Anikó Szilágyi, 2016

SCHOLARSHIP

Reflecting on Alice: A Textual Commentary on *Through the Looking-Glass*, by Selwyn Goodacre, 2016

Elucidating Alice: A Textual Commentary on *Alice's Adventures in Wonderland*, by Selwyn Goodacre, 2015

Behind the Looking-Glass: Reflections on the Myth of Lewis Carroll, by Sherry L. Ackerman, 2012

Selections from the Lewis Carroll Collection of Victoria J. Sewell, compiled by Byron W. Sewell, 2014

SOCIAL COMMENTARY

Clara in Blunderland, by Caroline Lewis, 2010

Lost in Blunderland: The further adventures of Clara, by Caroline Lewis, 2010

John Bull's Adventures in the Fiscal Wonderland, by Charles Geake, 2010

The Westminster Alice, by H. H. Munro (Saki), 2017

Alice in Blunderland: An Iridescent Dream,
by John Kendrick Bangs, 2010

SIMULATIONS

Davy and the Goblin, by Charles Edward Carryl, 2010

The Admiral's Caravan, by Charles Edward Carryl, 2010

Gladys in Grammarland, by Audrey Mayhew Allen, 2010

Alice's Adventures in Pictureland, by Florence Adèle Evans, 2011

Folly in Fairyland, by Carolyn Wells, 2016

Rollo in Emblemland, by J. K. Bangs & C. R. Macauley, 2010

Phyllis in Piskie-land, by J. Henry Harris, 2012

Alice in Beeland, by Lillian Elizabeth Roy, 2012

Eileen's Adventures in Wordland, by Zillah K. Macdonald, 2010

Alice and the Time Machine, by Victor Fet, 2016

Алиса и Машина Времени (Alisa i Mashina Vremeni),
Alice and the Time Machine in Russian, tr. Victor Fet, 2016

SEWELLIANA

Sun-hee's Adventures Under the Land of Morning Calm,
by Victoria J. Sewell & Byron W. Sewell, 2016

선희의 조용한 아침의 나라 모험기
(Seonhuiui Joyonghan Achim-ui Nala Moheomgi),
Sun-hee in Korean, tr. Miyeong Kang, 2017

Alix's Adventures in Wonderland:
Lewis Carroll's Nightmare, by Byron W. Sewell, 2011

Álobk's Adventures in Goatland, by Byron W. Sewell, 2011

Alice's Bad Hair Day in Wonderland, by Byron W. Sewell, 2012

The Carrollian Tales of Inspector Spectre, by Byron W. Sewell, 2011

The Annotated Alice in Nurseryland, by Byron W. Sewell, 2016

The Haunting of the Snarkasbord, by Alison Tannenbaum, Byron W. Sewell, Charlie Lovett, & August A. Imholtz, Jr, 2012

Snarkmaster, by Byron W. Sewell, 2012

In the Boojum Forest, by Byron W. Sewell, 2014

Murder by Boojum, by Byron W. Sewell, 2014

Close Encounters of the Snarkian Kind, by Byron W. Sewell, 2016

Translations

Кайкалдыҥ Јеринде Алисала болгон учуралдар (Kaykaldıñ Cerinde Alisala bolgon uçuraldar), *Alice* in Altai, tr. Küler Tepukov, 2016

Alice's Adventures in An Appalachian Wonderland, *Alice* in Appalachian English, tr. Byron & Victoria Sewell, 2012

Patimatli ali Alice tu Vãsilia ti Ciudii, *Alice* in Aromanian, tr. Mariana Bara, 2015

Алесіны прыгоды ў Цудазем'і (Alesiny pryhody u Tsudazem'i), *Alice* in Belarusian, tr. Max Ščur, 2016

На тым баку Люстра і што там напаткала Алесю (Na tym baku Liustra i shto tam napatkala Alesiu), *Looking-Glass* in Belarusian, tr. Max Ščur, 2016

Снаркаловы (Snarkalovy), *The Hunting of the Snark* in Belarusian, tr. Max Ščur, 2017

Crystal's Adventures in A Cockney Wonderland, *Alice* in Cockney Rhyming Slang, tr. Charlie Lovett, 2015

Aventurs Alys in Pow an Anethow, *Alice* in Cornish, tr. Nicholas Williams, 2015

Alice's Ventures in Wunderland, *Alice* in Cornu-English, tr. Alan M. Kent, 2015

Alices Hændelser i Vidunderlandet, *Alice* in Danish, tr. D.G., Forthcoming

آلیس در سرزمین عجایب (Âlis dar Sarzamin-e Ajâyeb),
Alice in Dari, tr. Rahman Arman, 2015

La Aventuroj de Alicio en Mirlando,
Alice in Esperanto, tr. E. L. Kearney (1910), 2009

La Aventuroj de Alico en Mirlando,
Alice in Esperanto, tr. Donald Broadribb, 2012

Trans la Spegulo kaj kion Alico trovis tie,
Looking-Glass in Esperanto, tr. Donald Broadribb, 2012

Les Aventures d'Alice au pays des merveilles,
Alice in French, tr. Henri Bué, 2015

Les Aventures d'Alice au pays des merveilles,
Alice in French, tr. Henri Bué, illus. Mathew Staunton, 2015

Alisanın Gezisi Şaşilacek Yerdä,
Alice in Gagauz, tr. Ilya Karaseni, 2017

ელისის თავგადასავალი საოცრებათა ქვეყანაში
(Elisis t'avgadasavali saoc'rebat'a k'veqanaši),
Alice in Georgian, tr. Giorgi Gokieli, 2016

Alice's Abenteuer im Wunderland,
Alice in German, tr. Antonie Zimmermann, 2010

Die Lissel ehr Erlebnisse im Wunnerland,
Alice in Palantine German, tr. Franz Schlosser, 2013

Der Alice ihre Obmteier im Wunderlaund,
Alice in Viennese German, tr. Hans Werner Sokop, 2012

Balþos Gadedeis Aþalhaidais in Sildaleikalanda,
Alice in Gothic, tr. David Alexander Carlton, 2015

Nā Hana Kupanaha a ʻĀleka ma ka ʻĀina Kamahaʻo,
Alice in Hawaiian, tr. R. Keao NeSmith, 2017

Ma Loko o ke Aniani Kū a me ka Mea i Loaʻa iā ʻĀleka ma Laila, *Looking-Glass* in Hawaiian, tr. R. Keao NeSmith, 2017

Aliz kalandjai Csodaországban,
Alice in Hungarian, tr. Anikó Szilágyi, 2013

Eachtra Eibhlíse i dTír na nIontas,
Alice in Irish, tr. Pádraig Ó Cadhla (1922), 2015

Eachtraí Eilíse i dTír na nIontas, *Alice* in Irish, tr. Nicholas Williams, 2007

Lastall den Scáthán agus a bhFuair Eilís Ann Roimpi,
Looking-Glass in Irish, tr. Nicholas Williams, 2009

Le Avventure di Alice nel Paese delle Meraviglie,
Alice in Italian, tr. Teodorico Pietrocòla Rossetti, 2010

Alis Advencha ina Wandalan,
Alice in Jamaican Creole, tr. Tamirand Nnena De Lisser, 2016

L's Aventuthes d'Alice en Êmèrvil'lie,
Alice in Jèrriais, tr. Geraint Williams, 2012

L'Travèrs du Mitheux et chein qu'Alice y dêmuchit,
Looking-Glass in Jèrriais, tr. Geraint Williams, 2012

Әлисәнің ғажайып елдегі басынан кешкендері
(Älïsäniñ ğajayıp eldegi basınan keşkenderi),
Alice in Kazakh, tr. Fatima Moldashova, 2016

Алисаның Хайхастар Чирінзер чорығы
(Alïsanıñ Hayhastar Çirinzer çorığı),
Alice in Khakas, tr. Maria Çertykova, 2017

Алисанын Кызыктар Өлкөсүндөгү укмуштуу окуялары
(Alisanın Kızıktar Ölkösündögü ukmuştuu okuyaları),
Alice in Kyrgyz, tr. Aida Egemberdieva, 2016

Las Aventuras de Alisia en el Paiz de las Maraviyas,
Alice in Ladino, tr. Avner Perez, 2016

לאס אב'ינטוראס די אליסייה אין איל פאאיס די לאס מאראב'ילייאס
(Las Aventuras de Alisia en el Paiz de las Maraviyas),
Alice in Ladino, tr. Avner Perez, 2016

Alisis pīdzeivuojumi Breinumu zemē,
Alice in Latgalian, tr. Evika Muizniece, 2015

Alicia in Terra Mirabili, *Alice* in Latin, tr. Clive Harcourt Carruthers, 2011

Aliciae per Speculum Trānsitus (Quaeque Ibi Invēnit),
Looking-Glass in Latin, tr. Clive Harcourt Carruthers, Forthcoming

Alisa-ney Aventuras in Divalanda, *Alice* in Lingua de Planeta (Lidepla), tr. Anastasia Lysenko & Dmitry Ivanov, 2014

La aventuras de Alisia en la pais de mervelias,
Alice in Lingua Franca Nova, tr. Simon Davies, 2012

Alice ẹhr Ẹventüürn in't Wunnerland,
Alice in Low German, tr. Reinhard F. Hahn, 2010

Contoyrtyssyn Ealish ayns Çheer ny Yindyssyn,
Alice in Manx, tr. Brian Stowell, 2010

Ko Ngā Takahanga i a Ārihi i Te Ao Mīharo,
Alice in Māori, tr. Tom Roa, 2015

Dee Erläwnisse von Alice em Wundalaund,
Alice in Mennonite Low German, tr. Jack Thiessen, 2012

Auanturiou adelis en Bro an Marthou,
Alice in Middle Breton, tr. Herve Le Bihan & Herve Kerrain, Forthcoming

The Aventures of Alys in Wondyr Lond,
Alice in Middle English, tr. Brian S. Lee, 2013

L'Avventure d'Alice 'int' 'o Paese d' 'e Maraveglie,
Alice in Neapolitan, tr. Roberto D'Ajello, 2016

L'Aventuros de Alis in Marvoland, *Alice* in Neo, tr. Ralph Midgley, 2013

Elises Eventyr i Undernes Land: den første norske *Alice*:
Elise's Adventures in the Land of Wonders: the first Norwegian *Alice*,
Alice in Norwegian, ed. & tr. Anne Kristin Lande, 2016

Æðelgýðe Ellendæda on Wundorlande,
Alice in Old English, tr. Peter S. Baker, 2015

La geste d'Aalis el Païs de Merveilles,
Alice in Old French, tr. May Plouzeau, 2017

Alitjilu Palyantja Tjuta Ngura Tjukurmankuntjala (Alitji's Adventures in Dreamland), *Alice* in Pitjantjatjara, tr. Nancy Sheppard, 2017

Alitji's Adventures in Dreamland: An Aboriginal tale inspired by *Alice's Adventures in Wonderland*, adapted by Nancy Sheppard, 2017

Alice Contada aos Mais Pequenos,
The Nursery "Alice" in Portuguese, tr., Rogério Miguel Puga, 2015

Соня въ царствѣ дива (Sonia v tsarstvie diva):
Sonja in a Kingdom of Wonder,
Alice in facsimile of the 1879 first Russian translation, 2013

Соня в царстве дива (Sonia v tsarstve diva),
An edition of the first Russian *Alice* in modern orthography, 2017

Охота на Снарка (Okhota na Snarka),
The Hunting of the Snark in Russian, tr. Victor Fet, 2016

La Aventures as Alice in Daumsenland,
Alice in Sambahsa, tr. Olivier Simon, 2013

Ocolo id Specule ed Quo Alice Trohv Ter,
Looking-Glass in Sambahsa, tr. Olivier Simon, 2016

'O Tāfaoga a 'Ālise i le Nu'u o Mea Ofoofogia,
Alice in Samoan, tr. Luafata Simanu-Klutz, 2013

Eachdraidh Ealasaid ann an Tìr nan Iongantas,
Alice in Scottish Gaelic, tr. Moray Watson, 2012

Alice's Adventchers in Wunderland,
Alice in Scouse, tr. Marvin R. Sumner, 2015

Mbalango wa Alice eTikweni ra Swihlamariso,
Alice in Shangani, tr. Peniah Mabaso & Steyn Khesani Madlome, 2015

Ahlice's Aveenturs in Wunderlaant,
Alice in Border Scots, tr. Cameron Halfpenny, 2015

Alice's Mishanters in e Land o Farlies,
Alice in Caithness Scots, tr. Catherine Byrne, 2014

Alice's Adventirs in Wunnerlaun,
Alice in Glaswegian Scots, tr. Thomas Clark, 2014

Ailice's Anters in Ferlielann,
Alice in North-East Scots (Doric), tr. Derrick McClure, 2012

Alice's Adventirs in Wonderlaand,
Alice in Shetland Scots, tr. Laureen Johnson, 2012

Ailice's Àventurs in Wunnerland,
Alice in Southeast Central Scots, tr. Sandy Fleemin, 2011

Ailis's Anterins i the Laun o Ferlies,
Alice in Synthetic Scots, tr. Andrew McCallum, 2013

Alice's Carrànts in Wunnerlan,
Alice in Ulster Scots, tr. Anne Morrison-Smyth, 2013

Alison's Jants in Ferlieland,
Alice in West-Central Scots, tr. James Andrew Begg, 2014

Alice muNyika yeMashiripiti,
Alice in Shona, tr. Shumirai Nyota & Tsitsi Nyoni, 2015

Алисаның қайғаллығ Черинде полған чоруқтары
(Alisanıñ qayğallığ Çerinde polğan çoruqtarı),
Alice in Shor, tr. Liubov′ Arbaçakova, 2017

Alis bu Cëlmo dac Cojube w dat Tantelat,
Alice in Ṣurayt, tr. Jan Beṯ-Ṣawoce, 2015

Alisi Ndani ya Nchi ya Ajabu, *Alice* in Swahili, tr. Ida Hadjuvayanis, 2015

Alices Äventyr i Sagolandet, *Alice* in Swedish, tr. Emily Nonnen, 2010

'Alisi 'i he Fonua 'o e Fakaofo',
Alice in Tongan, tr. Siutāula Cocker & Telesia Kalavite, 2014

Ventürs jiela Lälid in Stunalän, *Alice* in Volapük, tr. Ralph Midgley, 2016

Lès-avirètes da Alice ô payis dès mèrvèyes,
Alice in Walloon, tr. Jean-Luc Fauconnier, 2012

Anturiaethau Alys yng Ngwlad Hud, *Alice* in Welsh, tr. Selyf Roberts, 2010

I Avventur de Alìs ind el Paes di Meravili,
Alice in Western Lombard, tr. GianPietro Gallinelli, 2015

U-Alisi Kwilizwe Lemimangaliso,
Alice in Xhosa, tr. Mhlobo Jadezweni, 2017

Di Avantures fun Alis in Vunderland,
Alice in Yiddish, tr. Joan Braman, 2015

Alises Avantures in Vunderland,
Alice in Yiddish, tr. Adina Bar-El, Forthcoming

Insumansumane Zika-Alice,
Alice in Zimbabwean Ndebele, tr. Dion Nkomo, 2015

U-Alice Ezweni Lezimanga, *Alice* in Zulu, tr. Bhekinkosi Ntuli, 2014

www.ingramcontent.com/pod-product-compliance
Ingram Content Group UK Ltd.
Pitfield, Milton Keynes, MK11 3LW, UK
UKHW041826200726
13854UKWH00002BA/579

9 781782 011989